Coroner Creek

**Center Point
Large Print**

**This Large Print Book carries the
Seal of Approval of N.A.V.H.**

Coroner Creek

LUKE SHORT

CENTER POINT PUBLISHING
THORNDIKE, MAINE

This Center Point Large Print edition
is published in the year 2006 by arrangement with
Katherine Hirson and Daniel Glidden.

The text of this Large Print edition is unabridged. In other
aspects, this book may vary from the original edition. Printed in
Thailand. Set in 16-point Times New Roman type.

ISBN 1-58547-735-4

Library of Congress Cataloging-in-Publication Data

Short, Luke, 1908-1975.
    Coroner Creek / Luke Short.--Center Point large print ed.
        p. cm.
    ISBN 1-58547-735-4 (lib. bdg. : alk. paper)
    1. Large type books. I. Title.

PS3513.L68158C67 2006
813'.54--dc22

                                              2005027939

Coroner Creek

Chapter I

Some of the post lamps were out even before taps ended. As the last note of the bugle died, the dogs took it up, and their bedlam spread from the post to the agency dogs and was echoed far off by the curs around the clusters of wickiups on the reservation to the south.

It was a chorus of ferocity with an exquisite idiocy about it, and Chris Danning, knowing now he had been listening too intently, put his back against the wall of the trading post and settled into patience again. An Indian woman came out the door beside him, a sack of groceries slung over each shoulder, and tossed them into the bed of a spring wagon drawn up paralleling the trader's porch. She stepped in and drove off, and afterward the Apache buck came out. He stood in the rectangle of lamplight cast by the doorway, his shadow huge and almost formless in the dust of the road beyond, and scratched himself through a rent in his shirt, which was worn tails out. Afterward, he approached his pony at the tie rail, first regarding Danning's sorrel beside his own horse with a born horse stealer's admiration. He mounted and rode off after the wagon whose slack jolting was merging slowly into the distant racket of the dogs.

But even so, Danning heard the Indian's grunt of greeting to the approaching rider, and now Danning sat erect on the split-log bench against the store wall and waited. The rider barely touched the lamplight from the store before he was swallowed up in the darkness again, yet Danning recognized the scout. McCune had hunted Indians so long he rode like one, feet turned out and gently flailing.

Danning waited a precautionary moment, and then, when he was certain nobody was following McCune, he rose and stepped quietly through the doorway of the store. Even in the soft light cast by the lamp over the side counter there was something hard and angular about his high shoulders under the patched and weather-bleached calico shirt. Just inside the door was his saddle; he lifted it by the horn, looked briefly about the room and, seeing the trader, raised his hand in thanks and parting. His narrow face, sober to taciturnity, was blank with indifference; his gray eyes behind high and heavy cheekbones did not even wait to register the answering wave. He went out and saddled his horse swiftly, and rode west into the night after McCune.

The old scout was waiting well beyond the clutter of the agency buildings and the mission, and as Danning came up, McCune put his horse alongside at a walk.

"You bring your money?" McCune asked presently.

"You said to. Does that mean you've found one?"

"You're lucky," McCune murmured. "The buck wants to buy him a new wife. He's a Cherry-cow 'Pache, not one of these, or he wouldn't take your money."

"But he was in on the massacre?"

"He was in on it," McCune answered. "A trooper must of got to him because he's got a saber cut across his chest. Withered his arm."

They were silent now, and Danning checked his desire to question. The dimly seen wagon road still held the heat of the blazing Arizona day, and back at the agency some dog, surely stubborn, held to his senseless barking.

Presently, McCune put his horse off the wagon road and threaded his way carefully down a steep rock-strewn slope that presently leveled off in the sandy bed of a wash. McCune was waiting here, and when Danning came up, he said, "I better take your gun."

Danning handed it to him and McCune slipped it into his coat pocket and grunted. "It's hard to keep your temper if you ain't used to them. They brag, you know."

"I'll keep my temper."

"You better," McCune said gently. "I give my word."

They rode abreast down the wash for a couple of miles, climbed out of it and cut south across some sage flats and then came abruptly into a canyon in which a couple of small fires were burning some distance below. A dog picked them up and hounded them down the trail until McCune cursed it into silence. Afterward, on the level canyon floor, Danning saw the two brush wickiups, the tiny brush corral, and the garden plot contemptuously scratched in the poor earth beyond, which signified as permanent a home as the Apaches ever built. The smell of the camp, rising in the still warm night, was that of burning mesquite. They passed three women at the first fire, and McCune did not even look at them. Beyond, Danning saw the bucks. Their mesquite fire was not big and cast little light, so that the two Apaches hunkered between it and the other wickiup were shapes a man had to look for.

Before McCune dismounted he murmured a greeting which was returned almost inaudibly by one buck, and then he stepped out of the saddle and went across deliberately to squat beside the fire. He was a spare, bent man in a baggy, dusty black suit whose right pocket sagged with Danning's gun. Danning ground-haltered his horse and came up beside McCune and sat down, cross-legged.

McCune passed his sack of tobacco to the nearest Indian, who wore only a breechclout and shirt and was squatted comfortably on his heels, elbows on knees and arms straight out. He, Danning guessed, was not his man, and this was confirmed when the second Apache refused the tobacco. Danning knew that by taking it, the Indian would reveal the fact that under his filthy shirt his right arm was useless. Danning studied this man now, and was studied in return.

The buck did not bother to hide either his hatred or his contempt for the two white men, and Danning wondered at his own calmness. This Indian had been there, had seen it, had helped, had maybe done it, and yet Danning felt only a vast and imperturbable patience, no anger.

Presently McCune said, "Smoke up. This'll take time," and then began to talk to the Apaches in their language. The younger man, the stranger, kept watching Danning, his broad face, with its small, curved nose, stolid and sleepy and fierce even in repose.

The older Indian answered McCune now, and McCune waited until he had finished, and then said to Danning, "He wants to see the color of your money."

Danning took the buckskin bag containing two hundred dollars in eagles from his pocket and handed it to McCune, who tossed it to the young buck. He made no move to catch it, and let it lie at his feet.

Then McCune spoke again, and the younger buck answered at some length. McCune interrupted him only once before he finished.

McCune now said, turning to Danning: "He was with Tana the time Tana's bunch broke out of the reservation. Tana's scouts had picked up the paymaster's detail of Captain Jordan that was on its way from Grant to Pima Tanks, but they let it go through. They were after horses, but Jordan's horses weren't much and besides the detail was well armed. He says Tana never did know about the Quartermaster's train that was already at Pima Tanks with the load of rifles. His bunch was watching the paymaster's detail."

"Ask him the question," Danning said.

McCune spoke to the young Indian again, and was

answered at great length. Danning found himself leaning forward, trying to recognize a single word of the Apache's gibberish.

When the Indian finished, McCune said wryly to Danning, "He wants to brag first. Want to hear it?"

"Yes."

"Tana and his bunch were up in those dry hills to the west of Pima Tanks—Deaf Jensen's country—when that bad storm hit. It scattered their small *remuda* to hell-and-gone, and had most of 'em afoot. Tana figured it would be easier to raid for horses around Pima Tanks than to round up his own. He sent an old man— Sal Juan they called him—down into Pima Tanks, figuring Captain Jordan didn't know yet that Tana had broken out. Sal Juan was to hang around until Jordan's detail pulled out, and then Tana would raid the town. Sure enough Jordan hadn't got the word about Tana."

McCune turned now, and the Indian, without invitation, took up his story. Danning noticed McCune was listening with a still intentness, and he grunted as the Apache finished.

"In Pima Tanks," McCune continued then, "Sal Juan was braced by a white man he knew, a freighter. Said he had information Tana might want. Said he—"

"Ask his name," Danning interrupted.

McCune did. The Apache answered briefly, irritably. McCune said in a low voice, "He don't know it. Take it easy. Let him tell it."

The Apache spoke again, and while he was speaking, Danning heard a soft "Ah" from McCune,

14

and then the old scout translated.

"Sal Juan brought this white man out to the old sawmill and left him there, and went back and got Tana and another buck who could speak American and this son." McCune nodded his head toward the young buck who had been speaking. "The white man was in luck; he didn't know Tana'd broken out, but he knew Sal Juan was a friend of Tana's. When he met Tana, he made him this proposition. He said there was a Quartermaster train loaded with rifles in Pima Tanks. That train and a stage full of people and Captain Jordan's detail had all decided to throw in together and take the old road to Lincoln. That was through some bad Indian country, but they figured it wouldn't be dangerous now the 'Paches was quiet. Besides, they'd been held up by the storm too, and they was all in a hurry. The white man made this deal. In return for this information, Tana would raid the party when they was in Karnes Canyon. Tana could keep the horses and the rifles and ammunition. All the white man wanted was the pay chest in the back of Jordan's Daugherty wagon."

"Did he get it?" Danning said.

McCune nodded. "He got it. Tana's bunch cleaned out the picket line the first night. It took them three days to finish the job after that."

Danning's face did not alter as he heard this; his big hand lifted a little from his leg and then settled back again. He said in a dull, quiet voice, "Go back to the white man. Have him describe him. Everything he can

15

remember about him."

McCune leaned forward now, and he talked in short sentences and was answered in kind, and Danning, watching him, thought, *I've waited eighteen months for what he's going to tell me next,* and he wondered now at his own patience. It was a patience that had taken him a thousand miles, tirelessly tracking down the men at a half dozen scattered Army posts who had been first on the scene after the Karnes Canyon massacre. It had taken half a hundred laboriously written letters, and the patience to wait for their answers, which were always barren of the information he wanted. Until now, in a strange land, he was going to hear the words spoken by an Army scout he had not even known three days ago, and whom he would never see again after tonight.

McCune was finished now, and said to Danning, "Sal Juan knew him. The white man worked in the big post at Pima Tanks—Nohl and Johnson—freightin' for them. He was stocky, strong, maybe thirty, light curly hair, and dark brown eyes like an Injun's, with little hoods at the corners. He remembers the eyes most." McCune paused. "That what you want?"

"That's it."

Suddenly the Apache spoke, and McCune swiveled his head to listen. Danning, watching the buck, saw a sly kind of malice in his face. McCune then turned slowly and looked searchingly at Danning.

"What did he say?" Danning asked.

McCune answered quietly as he got to his feet.

"Nothin' you'd want to hear," and brushed the dust from his coat. He spoke his parting gravely to the two Apaches and they left the firelight for their horses.

They were on the dark flats again before their horses pulled abreast and then Danning asked, "Does this go to the Colonel?"

McCune was a long time answering. "I reckon not. It's water under the bridge except for the pay chest the renegade white got away with." He was silent a moment. "That was a few thousand dollars. Turn the story over to the Army and they spend five times that amount investigatin' and gettin' depositions and stirrin' up a bunch of 'Paches what wouldn't open their mouth about it anyway."

"Don't worry about the white man," Danning said.

They didn't speak again until they were on the wagon road, and then Danning reined up in the darkness.

McCune halted his horse and pulled his feet from the stirrups, folded his hands on the horn and spat. Then he said mildly, "Well, you leave me here, don't you?"

"Yes. What'd begin to pay you for your help?"

McCune grunted. "Forget it. Nothin'." He looked keenly in the darkness at Danning. "Maybe somethin' too. A question. If it's none of my business, tell me." He paused. "Was she your wife, son?"

"No. So that buck remembered her?"

"Your sister, maybe?"

"No. What did he say?"

McCune said quietly, without bitterness or outrage, "He has a silk dress from that raid, white like a wedding dress. He wondered if that's what you wanted."

Danning didn't say anything, and McCune reached in his pocket and hauled out Danning's gun and gave it to him.

Danning rammed it in the waistband of his trousers and then murmured, "She was on her way to marry me."

They parted after that, McCune heading back for the post, Danning riding on.

Chapter II

It was late summer when he came onto the flats below the Blackbow Range. He did not come in from the south over the mountains, which might have led to speculation, but from the dune country to the north, and he led a pack horse whose brand newly matched that of the sorrel he was riding. He came openly and camped on Coroner Creek the first night, and all the next day he looked upon the level brown grasslands of the Blackbow flats with the relief of a man who has lately come from the desert.

It was past suppertime, yet still light, when he entered the town of Triumph. It had been built on the flats at a bend of the Coroner, and a long level stretch of grass flats lay between it and the dark-timbered Blackbows hulking to the south.

He crossed the heavy bridge over the Coroner and faced the setting sun at the end of the long street, and the pitiless light of it seemed to take away the solidity of the frame stores flanking the wide and dusty street. Cowtown fashion, the bigger buildings crowded the four corners, and it was here he reined up in the slow evening traffic of the town, first looking down the street to his right and then to his left before he saw the archway of the feed stable. He turned left and passed the big hotel on the corner, and some doors beyond it he turned into the livery stable and dismounted.

He turned his horse into the corral in the rear, took his warbag from his pack, asked permission and received it of the hostler to leave his blankets and gear here, and sought the boardwalk, a tall, taciturn, sun-blackened man in tattered clothes, whose face was stern and forbidding.

The traffic of a summer evening stirred lazily on the streets, and Chris, remembering the hotel on the corner with the chairs on the flat railinged roof of its one-story veranda, turned toward it, warbag slung over his shoulder.

Ponies stood ranked in front of the big saloon opposite the hotel, and he let his gaze shuttle across the street.

The sign was there across the second building from the corner, and he paused, reading it.

MILES AND MCKEOGH, GENERAL M'CH'ND'SE

The name MILES was new, the white of the letters brighter, the black of the background darker than the rest of the sign. He thought without surprise, *He knew how to run a store, didn't he?* and stood there a moment, his bitter gray eyes reflective and without urgency. He let a pair of homeward-headed horses pull a spring wagon smartly past him, and then, his mind made up, he crossed the street and went into the store. Depositing his warbag by the door, he slowly cruised the aisles, watching for the face of the man whose description he had memorized. Presently he hauled up at the rear of the store before a door into a small office where there were two desks, a safe, and not much else. A young man with red hair looked up from a ledger and Chris asked, "Miles around?"

The man shook his head. "He spends most of his time out at the ranch. He's in mornings, usually."

Danning nodded and tramped out, and his disappointment was minor. A little more time didn't matter—was welcome, in fact.

Turning in at the hotel, he found the lobby deserted, and made his way across to the desk in the angle of the stairs.

Nobody was behind it, and yet Chris had the feeling that it was not long deserted. He waited a moment, looking past the worn chairs in the lobby through the big windows that looked out onto the main street and the cross street. Still nobody came, and then, spying the register before him, he turned it and signed his name. The keyboard hung beside the counter, and now he took a key from it, lifted his warbag and mounted the stairs which angled once before it lifted to the long corridor running lengthwise of the building.

At the head of the stairs he turned right and saw the numbers on the first and second doors, and he knew he was going in the wrong direction. About-facing, he only then saw the two women down the lamplit corridor coming toward him. One, the slightest of the two, had her arm about the waist of the second girl who seemed to Chris to be walking in her sleep. The slight girl had rich golden hair that may have once been done neatly atop her head, but which now straggled in wisps across her face. Even as Danning watched, the other girl staggered, and they both slammed abruptly against the wall.

Chris came toward them, and the slight girl, intent now on holding up her companion, looked up with a momentary surprise that washed out the distress in her face.

Chris said, "Can I help you?" and accepted the slow look of relief that came into the girl's face.

Chris bent and picked up the other girl, one arm under her knees, the other under her shoulder. Her head rolled back loosely against his shoulder, and he smelled the rich fragrance of her dark hair. And he smelled something else too, which was liquor.

The slight girl tried the nearest door and went in, stepping aside for Chris, who crossed the room and put down his burden on the bed. Standing over her, he looked at her a moment and in the fading evening light

21

he noticed that her face, young and pretty and pale as death now, had a kind of sulky defiance even in repose.

Chris glanced briefly at the girl beside him. She made no effort to tidy the wisp of hair that straggled down across her forehead and ear. She, too, had been watching the sleeping girl, and now she looked at Danning, this time more carefully, and her eyes, Chris noticed, were a pale brown, pale as old amber.

"You're new," she said.

Chris nodded.

"Do you know what's the matter with her?" the girl asked, inclining her head toward the girl on the bed.

"I'd say she was drunk," Chris answered. There was no censure in his voice, no interest either.

There was a faint bitterness in her that was reflected in her pale eyes as she nodded and glanced again at the sleeping girl. She bent over her now and put a hand on her shoulder. "Abbie, Abbie, wake up. Can you hear me?"

There was no pleading and no hysteria in her voice, and Chris sensed that she had done this before. She straightened and took a deep sighing breath that lifted her bosom under her plain blue dress. And now, almost absently, she tucked the stray strand of hair back in place and, looking at Chris, said, "Have you ridden far today? Eaten, too?"

The strangeness of her question held him mute a moment, and then she went on, "I need help with her. I've got to get her out of here and back to the ranch.

I—don't like to shame her by asking somebody she knows, and everyone knows her."

The bluntness of this girl and her sudden kindness lessened for an instant the deep taciturnity in him and he said, "I'll help you."

The girl put out her hand now. "I'm Kate Hardison."

Chris told her his name, removed his Stetson and took her small hand in his, and then she said, smiling only faintly, "Smoke a cigarette. We'll have to wait until it's darker."

She sank onto the edge of the bed, and Chris sat down stiffly in the rocker next the bed, put his worn and battered hat on the floor beside the chair and reached in his shirt pocket for his sack of tobacco dust. He did not speak, content now, as always, with silence. He fashioned and lighted a cigarette, and then leaned forward in his chair, elbows on knees, staring quietly at his cigarette, and he had the tranquility of a patient, patient man.

Kate Hardison studied him for perhaps a minute, and then she stood up and crossed over to the dresser and took a match from the tray and lighted the lamp. She put the lamp on the table beside the bed and said, "Her buggy is in the alley back of the hotel. When it's dark enough, you can carry her down to it and drive her out to Rainbow."

"Who do I ask for?"

"This is Mrs. Miles," Kate said. "They'll take her off your hands."

Something in his face must have revealed his surprise, for Kate said, "You didn't come here to work for Younger Miles, did you?"

"Younger Miles? No."

"Do you know him? Or anybody at Rainbow?"

"No. I'm a drifter."

Kate laughed shortly. "I don't mind calling Younger Miles a dog to his face. I have. It's just that it's bad manners to call him one to a person who might be a friend of his. If he has a friend," she added quietly.

Chris looked at the sleeping girl again, thinking, *So he bought a store with it and ranch with it and a drunken wife with it,* and then he looked down at his cigarette again, patient again.

Kate said, "She's pretty, isn't she?" and Chris started at the sound of her voice. He looked at her strangely and nodded, and Kate said, "She's good, too. Not like this. If it will make you feel repaid for this, you can believe that."

Chris was silent, and Kate, when he did not answer, said, "I think you can bring her now."

He lifted Abbie Miles in his arms, and Kate led the way down the corridor to the back stairs. They opened into the kitchen, dark now, and she opened the back door. A team haltered at the high loading platform and hitched to a top buggy swung their heads around in the near darkness to watch their approach. Chris gently set the girl in the buggy seat, and when he climbed over her and took his seat, she slumped heavily against him. Kate, speaking softly across Abbie Miles, said, "You can follow this alley south to the edge of town. The road takes you to the canyon of the Coroner and passes by Rainbow. The team will take you."

Chris picked up the reins.

"I'll wait up for you," Kate said.

Chris backed the team around and headed down the alley, and presently was on the main road south which pointed straight for the heart of the Blackbows.

He held the reins loosely in his big hands now and relaxed in the seat, thinking of the strangeness of his errand as he felt the girl's dead weight against his side and shoulder. *I've got his wife,* he thought. *I could kill her now if I were sure it would hurt him.* It gave him a feeling of power and he contrasted it with the months of helpless and hopeless bafflement that had ridden him ever since he got the few brief facts of the massacre from the Apache through McCune.

He was remembering, too, the weeks he had spent in Pima Tanks. When he had identified the long forgotten freighter by the name of Younger Miles who used to work for Nohl and Johnson, he was only a little farther along the trail he had to travel, for Miles was months gone, and nobody knew or cared where. It was in the second month there, when he had nothing to feed his anger except stubbornness, that he got the hint that had brought him here, a half summer's travel to the north. He had taken up his station in the saloon that morning, just as he did every morning, hoping against reason that something in the million words of barroom gossip he was ready to listen to would hold a clue to Miles' whereabouts. He had been the first customer, and he had listened to the two tattered swampers gossiping about customers as they cleaned up the saloon. One of them had spoken of the vanity of a Nohl and Johnson freighter in regard to boots he could not afford. Chris had listened and questioned, and when he learned the freighter they spoke of was Miles, he had written five bootmakers, expecting nothing. But one day a letter came. Yes, the Texas bootmakers said, they still made boots for Younger Miles, and they named this town.

So now he was almost finished. As full night came Chris thought of that with an odd tranquility—he was at the end of his search.

He heard the near horse whicker now and felt the pace of the buggy quicken, and moments later he saw the dark forms of several riders loom up ahead of him. They were traveling at the easy jog of men who had ridden long, and they broke ranks to let him pass through them.

And then, almost leisurely, one rider leaned out and caught the bridle of the near horse and pulled the team to a stop, calling, "You all right, Mrs. Miles?"

Chris said, "She's all right," and watched the four riders pause at this strange voice; then, as one, they put their horses up to the buggy. A match was wiped alight on the trouser leg of the rider nearest Chris, and then he was squinting into the glare of it, looking at a young puncher whose mouth was going slack with surprise. The match died and the puncher said wonderingly, "Who the hell is that?" just as a man on the other side struck another match. He held it close to Abbie Miles and said disgustedly, "She's drunk, Ernie,"—and Chris shuttled his glance to the brand on the man's horse. It was three concentric half circles, and he knew this would be Rainbow and that he was not breaking faith with Kate Hardison in letting these men see Abbie Miles.

He said, "I'm taking her home," and waited, while the match died.

Ernie was the man who had stopped the team. Now he pulled his horse up alongside and flicked a match alight with his thumbnail. Chris saw a big man whose bleak eyes in his long and narrow face regarded him briefly, dispassionately.

"So she lets strangers get her drunk now," he said in a soft Texas voice. "Get out of that buggy."

"I'll talk from here."

"Get out of there or I'll kick you out," Ernie said flatly.

The match flame wavered and faded, and in that instant Chris knew that Ernie meant what he said. He knew, too, that the sudden darkness after the match flame died would mean a moment of blindness for the Texan, and when the match guttered out, he gathered his feet beneath him, dropped the reins and hurled his body at the black bulk on the saddle beside him.

His near shoulder caught Ernie in the chest and he wrapped his arm around his neck, locking his head in the crook of his arm. They fell off the horse that way, on their sides, Chris' weight dragging them to the ground. The breath was driven from Ernie in a great grunt, but he fought immediately, strongly, trying to bring his knee up into Chris' groin. Chris rolled away from him and they both came to their feet, Chris an instant sooner than the Texan, and he lunged again, this time swinging savagely and blindly in the dark. His first blow caught Ernie in the face, but Ernie came on, grappling with him, and they fell locked in each other's arms. The nearest Rainbow rider was calling the others.

Ernie was on him now, slugging great sledging blows at his face and chest. Now he half rolled over, swinging his arm up and catching Ernie around the chest. He rolled the rest of the way then, and Ernie came down with him. They were both on their sides, hitting blindly and futilely at each other when the Rainbow crew landed on them.

Chris felt his arms seized, and he was dragged off Ernie, fighting stubbornly against his two captors. They hauled him to his feet and he struggled silently, raging, and then subsided, breathing deeply. He heard the third man haul Ernie to his feet, and Ernie said thickly, "Get a fire built."

While the third man beat out in the mesquite brush alongside the road for fuel, Chris waited for what was coming. His anger was steady, unspent. The puncher returned with an arm-full of dry brush, threw it in the road, tramped it to kindling and touched a match to it. In its mounting flare, Chris saw Ernie standing spraddle-legged and hatless, his shirt ripped half off him, one hand on his hip. With his other hand and sleeve, he was wiping away the blood steadily dripping from his nose, and his bleak eyes were baleful and wicked. Chris, seeing it, crowded him.

"You build up a big enough fire and we'll finish it," Chris invited. He tried to shake off the man on either arm, but they held him.

Ernie didn't say anything immediately, and in that pause Chris saw his indecision.

Ernie said, "What are you doing with Mrs. Miles?"

Chris told him curtly of Kate Hardison's request, and Ernie said slowly, "That better be so."

It was over, Chris knew.

One of the men holding him, a squat barrel of a man whose round legs almost split his trousers, said, "You never gave her a drink?"

"She's been that way since I saw her."

Ernie grunted and turned and went over to the buggy and looked in the seat. When Chris had jumped, Abbie Miles had fallen on her side in the buggy seat. She lay there, still asleep.

Ernie turned and looked speculatively at Chris, and then said, "I reckon we've made a mistake. Let him go."

The two men took their hands off Chris, and Ernie said, "Ray, you drive her home. I'll bring your horse."

A wiry middle-aged puncher took over the reins, and Chris accepted his gun the Rainbow hand offered him, and rammed it in the waistband of his pants. The team was driven on, and Ernie said to Chris, "Take his

29

horse," and went over to his own mount. Chris stepped into the saddle of the extra horse and fell in with the others, and they headed back across the flats toward Triumph. He knew Ernie was unforgiving and unafraid, and that his pride would not let him drop this here. Besides, he had given away a secret that should have been kept.

Ernie's soft Texas drawl broke the silence presently. He tried to make it pleasant. "Ridin' through, or do you figure to drift?"

"Haven't made up my mind yet."

"We're short-handed at Rainbow," Ernie said. "If you figure to stay, think it over. Miles is a good boss, and about tonight—well, I reckon I made a mistake."

This was a concession, Chris knew, and yet there was not a jot of apology in Ernie's soft voice.

Chris said, "I'll think it over."

They fell silent. To the east the light of a ranch showed briefly, then was lost behind a tangle of corrals, and soon they were in sight of the lights of Triumph.

And Chris waited for the rest. When it came, Ernie was open enough about it.

"Mrs. Miles is worried, I reckon. Her father is goin' to die, and she knows it. He's sheriff." Ernie paused long enough to let that, and its implication, sink in. "So if she drinks some whisky once in a while, it's nobody's business but Rainbow's. Nobody's."

Chris turned this over in his mind, and then said quietly, "I don't talk about a woman." And he added just

30

as bluntly, "But if I wanted to, you wouldn't stop me."

He saw Ernie's head swivel toward him but nobody said anything. They were on Triumph's main street now, and when they were abreast the hotel, Chris pulled up and dismounted. Ernie reached down for the reins of his horse and Chris handed them to him. Their glances met briefly, and Ernie's pale eyes held neither dislike nor respect. He had done a necessary job within the limits of caution, and he was ready for any consequence. He said equably, "Remember Rainbow if you're looking for a ridin' job."

"I will," Chris said, and Ernie pulled Chris' horse away.

Chris went into the lobby. A puncher was asleep on the sofa against the wall, hat over his eyes against the light from the overhead kerosene lamp, and a pair of townsmen were playing checkers at a table against the wall. Chris took the key from his pocket and consulted the number on its tag, and went upstairs to his room. He lighted the lamp and found his warbag on the chair. Kate Hardison had evidently seen his name on the register.

Stripping off his shirt, he sloshed water from the pitcher into the bowl, and had his upper body soaped when the knock came on the door.

Kate Hardison's voice followed immediately. "Come down for supper when you're through."

"All right," Chris said, and went back to the washing. The soap smarted in his knuckles and he glanced down and found a couple of them skinned

31

rawly. Afterward, he put on a clean shirt from his warbag, and then looked in the mirror. He ran a hand over the black swirl of a two-day beard stubble, and then combed his ragged black hair. Finished, his hands sank slowly to his sides, and the images that had been ribboning through his mind this while took shape, and he thought, *If I work for him, I can pick the time and the place to kill him. And tell him why.*

A minute afterward, he turned down the lamp and descended the stairs, his body slack with weariness and hunger.

There was a lamp on a rear table in the dining room, a place set by it. Kate Hardison poked her head through the kitchen door, and by the time he was seated, she was bringing him the food. A platter of steaks, and bread—because she knew he would be tired of biscuits—and potatoes, with thick juice gravy, a double wedge of green-apple pie and a plate of pale butter and a pot of coffee were set before him.

She left him, and came back only when the edge was off his appetite. Pouring herself a cup of black coffee, she took a chair opposite him, and as he reached for his sack of tobacco he looked up and surprised her watching him.

Kate Hardison said, "You couldn't have made Rainbow. Who did you meet?"

"The crew," Chris said. "They took over."

"Which one of them did you hit?"

Chris looked up quickly, and when he saw her glance level upon him, he knew she'd seen his knuckles. He wiped the edge of his cigarette across his tongue and put it in the corner of his lips and said, "Ernie somebody."

Kate only looked at him searchingly and laughed then. It was a real laugh, too, with an inexpressible merriment in it that puzzled Chris, who watched her unsmilingly.

"Everybody wants to hit Ernie and nobody does," Kate explained. "People with reason, I mean."

He said nothing, and Kate said, with a sudden shrewdness, "He thought you'd got her drunk, didn't he?"

"Something like that."

"Whoever is giving her whisky is going to get hurt," Kate said.

Chris touched a match to his cigarette and inhaled deeply, and he felt an obscure irritation. But he was indifferent to Mrs. Miles' habits, and once more his thoughts settled back into the gray taciturnity of habit. He knew Kate Hardison had poured her coffee and sat down across from him because she wanted to talk, and yet he could feel no interest in her. Somewhere along the line he had lost the knowledge of the social niceties; he knew of nothing he wanted to say to this girl, pleasant as she was. He studied the table, musing, indifferent, not even knowing he was doing so, and he was lost in his gray contemplation.

When he heard her chair scrape, he yanked his attention back to the present. She was standing, collecting the dishes. He rose and took his share, and followed her back into the kitchen. It was a spacious place, clean, with a massive shining black range against the back wall.

He said, out of the desire to appear friendly, "You run this hotel yourself?"

"Everything but the cooking and cleaning. That doesn't leave much."

Her voice was now reserved and cold: she had wanted to be friendly, and had been rebuffed and had accepted it. He would have liked to tell her that he'd meant nothing by his silence, that it didn't matter, that he was only part of a man and not what she thought, that the only thing in the world he wanted was to kill a man, and that his waking hours were spent in pondering how that death could be made an exquisite agony.

When she was finished tidying up, he followed her through the dining room and into the lobby. She paused at the sofa where the puncher was sleeping, hesitated a moment, and then turned again to Chris. "I hate to wake him. Would you help me once more?"

Chris nodded, and she went ahead of him up the stairs. She waited for him at the head and explained in a quiet voice, "My father is bedridden from a fall several years ago, but he spends all day on the gallery so he can be outdoors. Fred, the man asleep down there, helps me move him in each night, but I didn't want to wake him tonight."

At the first door of the corridor she went in, Chris

following. It was a big corner living room, comfortable with bright curtains and rugs and furniture worn with use.

Kate opened the wide door that let out onto the gallery and Chris followed her out.

The gallery was unroofed and open to the sky, railinged its length, and there were some chairs and a table here. Under the window on a pallet faintly lighted by the lamp inside lay a man who had once been big. Even now he was not thin, but the erosion of age had started. His hair was white, clipped short, like his even mustache, and the sun and the weather had browned his skin deeply and bleached his hair. He had sharp, uncomplaining eyes, and when Kate said, "This is a new one, Walt—Chris Danning," he smiled and held out a firm brown hand.

Chris shook hands and Kate's father said immediately, dryly, "So you're the hand Ernie Coombs wants for Rainbow? How are you, son?"

Chris looked soberly at him and said, "You've got good ears, Mr. Hardison."

"A cripple's pastime," Hardison said, without rancor.

"If you come to see him tomorrow, he'll know your footsteps before he sees you," Kate said, and she smiled fondly at her father.

Hardison said, "I said that about Ernie because I've been tryin' to figure it out since I saw you." He hesitated. "You don't look like a Rainbow hand, somehow."

"He's not," Kate said bluntly. "Mr. Danning beat up Ernie tonight, and Ernie would rather have him with him than against him."

Hardison grunted and looked searchingly at Chris, who shifted his feet faintly. "What'll you do, son?"

"Likely take it. My stake's gone."

He felt Kate's glance on him, and could even feel the reproof in it, but he did not look at her.

"There are other outfits," Kate said quickly.

"None that's offered me a job."

"Don't peck at him," Hardison said gently to Kate. "A man's got to get his feet on the ground. How's Abbie?"

"Home. Want to go in now?"

Hardison nodded, and Chris took the head of his pallet, Kate the foot. They carried him through the living room to the small bare bedroom beyond, and Chris was aware that a small anger was riding Kate. He could see it in the set of her wide lips, and he knew that she felt in some obscure way he had betrayed her confidence. She had asked him if he was going to work for Miles, and he'd said no; two hours later, he'd said yes. It troubled him faintly that he couldn't tell her why he'd changed his mind, and then he thought, with the old selfishness, *Why should I care what she thinks?*

He said good night to Walt Hardison and trailed Kate back through the living room to the corridor door. He noticed now for the first time that she was wearing a different dress, a green one with long sleeves and collar edged in a fine line of white lace that made her skin seem faintly golden. The fact that he had even noticed it surprised him, but now it was too late to even look at her; she was standing with the door open, unsmiling.

"Thank you for both your favors," she told him, and he waited for that half smile, and it did not come and he went out.

Kate paused a moment by the closed door, and then walked slowly back into the bedroom.

"Surly devil," she said, almost angrily, and glanced over at her father. He winked solemnly, and suddenly she laughed. "All right, Walt. Only he is."

"A good many men are."

"But when I asked him to help me this afternoon, he seemed so willing. I even asked him if he was going to work for Younger, and when he said he wasn't I gave Younger a cussing out."

"He can change his mind."

"Yes, but—" She paused, frowning in concentration, and then she shrugged. "I guess what I'm really mad about is that he went against my advice."

She went over to the chest of drawers against the wall, on top of which was a scattering of books, a pair of pipes, and a small size crock with a lid. She picked up one of the pipes, packed it expertly with tobacco from the crock, tamping down the load with a match. Then she put the pipe in her mouth, struck a match and lighted the tobacco, and when the pipe was drawing nicely, she handed it to her father. She retained a little

37

of the smoke in her mouth, and blew it out gently, critically.

Her father watched her with the faint amusement which this nightly ritual always afforded him.

Now she sat down on the edge of the pallet, elbows on knees and regarded him thoughtfully. "What's wrong with him?"

"Who? Danning?" Her father smoked a moment, and then said, "I dunno. His spirit is deader than my legs. You can see it in his eyes."

"They're ugly. The rest of his face isn't. He just doesn't care."

"Then why should you?"

Kate couldn't answer that, and wished she could.

Chapter III

Chris ate an early breakfast at a restaurant up the cross street and then cruised the other direction looking for a barbershop. He passed under the gallery of the hotel, and a swamper at the saloon across the street quit sloshing water on the boardwalk while he passed, giving him good morning.

Beyond, the stores were opening up, and ahead, a clerk sweeping the boardwalk was in a good-natured wrangle with the aproned bartender in the doorway of a saloon across the street. The new sun laid a long shadow behind the clerk, and the dust he stirred raised a bright moted plume at the edge of the walk in the quiet morning air.

While the barber shaved Chris and cut his hair, the Negro boy carried hot water for his bath in the back room. Chris gave him money and sent the boy out to buy a new shirt and afterward lay in the steaming water that filled the zinc tub. Presently the boy returned with the shirt, putting it on the chair with his clothes, and said, "Miss Hard'son says you be sure and stop to see her 'fore you go."

Chris told him to keep some of the money, and when the boy was gone he sat musing, the soap in his hand, his glance still on the door. *Is she afraid I'll tell the town about Mrs. Miles?* he thought irritably, and he was surly and intolerant of anything that could distract him now when nothing must, and he knew he was.

He dressed, putting on his blue calico shirt, and he combed down his wet hair. Afterward he picked up his gun, opened the loading gate and spun the cylinder, counting the loads. He rammed it in the waistband of his pants and put on his Stetson and went out, settling his score. Outside, the morning traffic of the town was stirring, and he teetered on the edge of the boardwalk and observed it while he rolled and lighted a cigarette, and then turned downstreet again. Nothing remained but to pick up his warbag and ride out to Rainbow, for he had made his decision.

He passed the big saloon with its corner entrance and paused on the boardwalk to let a pair of riders pass him. Lifting his glance to the hotel gallery across the way he saw Kate Hardison and some other women

39

there, and supposed they were talking to Kate's father.

He was standing thus when he heard his name called from behind him. "Danning."

It came to him that this was one of Ernie's crew, and he turned and saw three men standing in the recessed doorway of the saloon. He recognized the man in the middle as Miles' bookkeeper by his red hair, and his attention shifted to the slight, sallow old man beside him on whose loose, buttonless vest the star of the Sheriff's office was pinned. And then the third man raised a hand and beckoned, and Chris looked at him.

The recognition came without shock but with the full weight of conviction, like the massive ridgepole timber of a barn being slipped into place: *Stocky, strong, maybe thirty, light curly hair, and dark brown eyes like an Indian's, with little hoods at the corners.* The Apache's words, through McCune, that he had remembered each day anew. The little folds of flesh on the corner of the upper eyelid were pronounced, giving Younger Miles an air of sleepy benevolence. He had grown a mustache, a silky chestnut color, and it bisected his square face. The hair at his temples was fair; the shape of his body under his black suit was blocky, and yet he was taller than Chris had pictured him.

He thought, without any excitement, *I could kill him now,* but when Miles' hand dropped to his side, Chris wheeled and came toward him. A cold and evil knowledge that the time and the place were of his naming now made him obey.

He halted in front of the three, his face impassive, and Younger Miles, sizing him up briefly, said, "I'm Younger Miles. Ernie says you can't make up your mind about workin' for me."

Chris hesitated, and then said gently, "That's what I told him."

"If I pay a man," Younger said idly in a low voice, "he'll be loyal enough to me to shut his mouth. The other kind I don't trust."

"And if you don't pay him?"

"We'll see you to your horse," Miles said.

The husband and the father, Chris thought, and he stepped back to look at them, and wild and reckless anger took him. A puncher strolled behind him, turning the corner, and now Chris raised his voice and said to the puncher, "Hold on a minute, friend."

The puncher looked over his shoulder, saw he was spoken to, and halted.

"Do you know Mrs. Miles?" Chris asked.

The florid-faced puncher looked at Chris and then shuttled his glance to Younger Miles and nodded in hesitant greeting, and said, "Yes."

Chris said, "I took her home last night. She was drunk—dead drunk."

The puncher's mouth came open and he looked furtively at Miles and turned and hurried off.

Chris didn't see him; he was watching Younger Miles, and the rage in him was hot and he could taste it in his mouth.

The shock was held in Younger Miles' eyes a

41

fleeting moment, and then the anger came blazing up. It came far enough that Chris thought, *Now it'll happen,* and he backed up another step, waiting.

Miles' face had gone gray now with his anger, and yet there was a puzzlement in his eyes too. He waited a long, dragging moment, and then said quietly, "You'll regret that," and turned and walked into the saloon.

Chris turned too, and he was in the street before he heard the voice of the Sheriff rise in tired anger, "Come back here!"

Chris didn't even pause. He walked leisurely across the street and traveled under the hotel gallery and went into the hotel. He felt calm and without anger, clean as rain. He waited a moment in the empty lobby to see if the Sheriff would follow him and, when nothing happened, he turned and tramped up the stairs.

Rounding the turn, he looked up and saw Kate Hardison standing at the landing. He saw the frightened wonder in her eyes as she stood aside, and he halted at the head of the stairs. "The boy said you wanted to see me."

"Not any more," Kate said. She couldn't keep the shakiness of anger out of her voice now. "How could you do that? How could you?"

Chris said blankly, "What?"

"What has Abbie Miles done to you that you'd tell that to the whole town? What has she?" Kate demanded angrily.

The realization came slowly to him then. He had to reach for it behind his obsession and his recklessness that gripped him still, and he stared at her, and the puzzlement slowly faded from his face.

"You're a cruel damned man!" Kate said hotly. "I hope he gets you!"

She turned her back to him and went out the corridor door that let onto the gallery. When she was gone Chris went down the hall to his room and closed the door behind him.

He stood there a moment, and slowly took off his hat and threw it on the bed. *I could have got him then, but I want him to know why,* he thought. And then he acknowledged to himself that he had made a mistake. He should have held his temper and accepted Miles' ultimatum, which he had planned to accept anyway. And while he mused thus, Kate's words kept crowding into his mind, "You're a cruel damned man!"

He sat on the bed now, hands clasped loosely before his knees, and a strange shame took hold of him. The puncher he'd stopped would repeat the story, and if Kate had heard him from the gallery, so had others. He had not meant to hurt Abbie Miles, but his unthinking recklessness had done so. It came to him then, as it had come to headstrong men before him, that revenge was never completely personal, for other people got hurt, and they were the wrong people.

But to that thought only his black stubbornness answered, and he rose and looked about him. He

43

would have to move now. Younger Miles was hardly a man to wait, and when the showdown came Chris did not want a town at his back. He wanted country and freedom to move, where the hunter and the hunted were equal.

He was ramming his few personal belongings into his warbag when the knock came on the door. Kate, he thought, and he went across the room and opened the door.

There was a girl he had never seen before standing there. She was tall, and wore a divided skirt, calf-skin vest and scuffed work-softened boots. Her low-crowned Stetson was dangling from her hand by its chin strap, and her brown hair was parted at one side and done in a thick club in the back. She had eyes of a deep violet blue, and they studied Chris now with a sober good humor.

"I heard you from the gallery," she said. "May I come in?"

Chris wordlessly opened the door and stepped back, and she walked past him into the room. Her face, Chris noticed as she passed him, had a strange and becoming freshness from the side, a short, straight nose and full lips that were faintly curled at the corners, like a child's. Her low, rounded cheekbones held a brushing of color.

She stopped abruptly when she saw his open warbag at the foot of the bed, and she turned and said, "So you're leaving?"

Chris only nodded, and the girl looked gravely at

44

him. "Younger Miles is afraid of you, isn't he?"

"He's not used to me," Chris said dryly.

"No, he's afraid. He's never taken that from any man."

Chris didn't answer; he felt a quickening impatience to be out of here.

The girl sensed it, for she said, "I won't keep you long, and I'll make it plain. I want you to work for me."

Chris was shaking his head in negation even before she finished, and he did not know why.

"So you're drifting," the girl said. She sat down on his bed now and studied him carefully a moment. "Stop and think what I'm offering you. If you stay in the open here you'll be dogged by Rainbow until you make the fight. They can do it, you know, because Younger Miles is Sheriff O'Hea's son-in-law. How'll you do it alone?"

"I hadn't thought."

"It's time to. You're fair game when you hit the street."

Chris was silent, considering this. He hadn't thought that far ahead, and yet the girl had outlined his position accurately.

"Who are you?" he asked finally.

"Della Harms. Our place is the Box H, out on the Blackbow flats. My mother and I run it with three hands. If you're touchy about working for women, don't be. On a steer's hip our Box H brand may look like a Henhouse, and a lot of people call it that, but it's run like any man's ranch."

She smiled faintly but Chris didn't see it. Three men,

45

she had said. That would put something at his back, and that was all he needed. But—what was she after?

He said, "What's the trade, Della?"

"Nobody's stopped Rainbow yet. I think you might."

"Stopped it?" Chris asked curiously.

"Yes. Stopped Younger Miles. He's hungry, and he was born hungry, I think. He's got money, and he's getting more, just as fast as the hundred deals he's got on the fire come to a boil. Where money won't work, he's got a rough crew, and where the crew won't work he's got the still, small voice of the sheriff. It makes the right noise at the right time. It's hard on the rest of us, and it's only a year and a half old. I just want to stop it."

Chris regarded her curiously, sensing the ambiguity and lightness of her words covered something more serious. "Why you?" he asked.

"He's starting with us," she said soberly. "He's been slow, but he's coming." She was silent a moment. "Younger wants everything down in black and white. If you can show a deed for anything, he wants to buy it. If you can't, he offers to share it with you. Say it's open range we're talking about, range you've used and that custom has made yours. Younger will have a hundred head in ahead of you, because the range is open." She shrugged. "He's too big to tangle with, and you haven't got title anyway. You let him have it."

It came to Chris now that Della had just answered something for him, and he recalled the hundred

46

nights when he had planned the death of Younger Miles. It wasn't to be a clean, swift death. He wanted to repay in kind those three nights of terror that Bess Thornley had lived through at Karnes Canyon before her death. This was his obsession, that those three nights and days when she saw the hopelessness of escape, the wedding that would never take place, the man she was never to have, the children she was never to hold, the years of living that must be telescoped into the lonely, fearful and vanishing minutes before death, must not go unavenged. And now this girl who was watching him so carefully had given him the answer. It had been there all along, so close he hadn't seen it. Younger Miles had turned renegade and betrayed and killed for money and the things money would bring him, nothing more, so that it was precious to him beyond all else. Strip him of that and you killed his dreams as surely as those three days and nights at Karnes Canyon had killed Bess' dreams. Only after that was done was it right for Younger Miles to die.

The decision must have been reflected in his face, for Della Harms said, "You'll come."

Chris nodded. "I'll draw lightning, Della."

"I know that, and I don't care." She put out her hand and Chris took it. Della said then, "Throw your stuff in the buckboard out front. We'll be going as soon as you're ready." She went to the door, opened it and paused and turned to look at him, and there was a shrewdness in her eyes as she said, "You haven't given much of a damn about anything for a long time, have you, Chris?"

"No."

"You'll have to start. You'll have to care about Box H, because it's our life."

"I've always worked for my pay, Della."

She nodded and went out, and he put the last of his belongings in his warbag, slung it over his shoulder and tramped downstairs. Kate Hardison was behind the desk, apparently waiting for him, and he laid a coin on the counter and received his change, all in silence. As he stooped to pick up his warbag again, Kate asked, "Are you going to work for Della and her mother?"

Chris nodded. "That why you sent the boy to get me?"

"That's why," Kate said in an unfriendly voice. "I'm sorry now I did. I would think you'd see why it won't work too."

"Last night," Chris said tonelessly, "you didn't want me to work for Rainbow. Now you don't want me to work for Box H. What would suit you?"

"If you'd ride on through," Kate said flatly.

They regarded each other with something close to dislike in their eyes, and then Chris said, "A man never lacks for advice from you, does he?"

That touched her; she leaned both elbows on the counter and inclined her head. "I'll take that, if I can give this. Have you stopped to think what you're bringing Della and her mother?"

"Younger Miles? He's decided that already," Della said.

"But not the way they'll get it with you there."

"That's a risk I named and she accepted."

"And that doesn't lessen it," Kate said immediately. And she added with an open malice, "You have a talent for using completely helpless women, haven't you?"

"Did I use you, or help you?"

Kate blushed deeply, and straightened up. "I've thanked you for that but I won't again. Good-by."

Chapter IV

Ernie Coombs came out of the timber along the upper trail above Rainbow around eight o'clock that morning. He'd already taken a look at the line shack his men were throwing up in Thessaly Canyon and had dropped off some salt in the Aspen meadows. Now he gave his big bay its head and let it pick its own footing down the steep trail that came into the ranch at the end of the horse pasture. Ernie felt a driving man's satisfaction in getting a lot done while the day was young, but this satisfaction was tempered somewhat as he looked down at Rainbow.

The name, he thought, was a mockery. Tucked away in this narrow canyon, the sun hadn't touched it yet, and Ernie, who'd been riding in the sun a couple of hours, hunched his heavy shoulders with expectant chill. The big new two-story frame house below him, almost square and freshly shingled and painted white, looked cold and far too grand, and it vaguely affronted Ernie's practical mind. It lay almost on the bank of hurrying Coroner Creek, leaving room only for a narrow yard before it abutted the steep side of the timbered mountain. Up the narrow valley from it and still on this side of the creek lay the solid log ranch buildings and corrals, and these pleased Ernie more. The new bridge, its peeled timbers still yellow, spanned the river between the house and the outbuildings, and even at this three hundred feet above the house Ernie could hear the din of the river.

He came off the trail at the pasture gate and, hearing a rhythmic pounding at the blacksmith shop, put his horse across the grassless barn lot and reined up at the weathered, sloping-roofed shed.

Arch Oatman stopped hammering on the wagon felloe and looked up at the big foreman.

"She up yet?" Ernie said.

"Ain't asked."

"Then quit the racket," Ernie said flatly. "A bear couldn't sleep through that."

Arch was a tall, morose-looking puncher, but docile enough; he put down his sledge, spat, and, as he tucked in the tail of his sun-faded shirt, observed with a disarming mildness, "You'd sleep through a fire if you went to bed with the load she did. So would I."

A faint anger fanned in Ernie's bleak eyes, and then vanished immediately. How could you keep a crew respectful if they were asked to carry the boss' wife home dead drunk? He said, "I know, but take it easy. Where's Younger?"

"Town."

Ernie grunted and put his horse toward the bridge. He regarded the fantastic gingerbread house on his right now with a hard disapproval as he crossed the bridge and picked up the road on the opposite bank of the Coroner and turned toward Triumph. The thought of that pretty woman there and her drunkenness both outraged and baffled him, for Ernie was a simple man, tough and direct as a boyhood on the trail drives and in trail towns could make him. Abbie Miles was a rich man's wife, with a paid housekeeper and cook, a "good woman." Yet "good women" didn't drink themselves drunk, and that fact tormented Ernie, tarnishing the pride he had in everything Rainbow. He had a lot of respect for Younger, but it was tempered with a private reservation. A real man wouldn't put up with that.

Soon he was out of the shadow of the mountain so that the sun came cheerfully through the foothill pines and presently, leaving the Coroner, he dropped down onto the grass flats before Triumph.

On this straight stretch of road the sun was dazzling, the day already warm. Ernie peeled his jumper off his sloping, powerful shoulders and tied it to the cantle, and looked off to the sun-drenched reaches of the flats abutting the Blackbows to the east. Then ahead of him he saw the buckboard and the two horses, one with rider, approaching. It wasn't long before he identified

the buckboard as belonging to Della Harms and minutes later, when he'd passed the wagon road that
turned off to the Coroner and Box H beyond, he recognized the rider as the drifter he'd tangled with last
night.

For a moment he couldn't associate the drifter with
Della Harms, and then it came to him. The drifter was
leading the pack horse, so he was likely headed over
the Blackbows through the valley of the Coroner.
He'd leave Della Harms at the turnoff and head up the
valley to camp up in the high timber tonight or else
put up at Bije Fulton's Hotel at Station. Tomorrow
he'd be over the pass and out of the country, a man
who'd been braced, and chose to drift rather than
work.

Ernie sat arrogantly in the saddle as he approached
them, as befitted the foreman of Rainbow. The drifter
was riding next the off horse; Ernie unsmilingly
touched his hat to Della Harms, and then his gaze
shuttled to the drifter. He felt again, as he had felt last
night when he looked into the gray eyes of this man, a
faint uneasiness; he nodded and thought, *You may be
tough, brother, but we put you on the run,* and when he
was past them he settled a little more slackly in the
saddle.

Triumph was astir now, and Ernie put his horse in at
the tie rail in front of the store and dismounted stiffly.
He tramped down the store's main aisle to the office at
the rear where MacElvey was seated at a rolltop desk
by the window, his head, with its fiery thatch of red

hair, bent over some papers.

Ernie leaned against the doorjamb and rammed both thumbs in the waistband of his pants. There was a faint scorn in his bleak eyes as he regarded the crowded and untidy office that was MacElvey's and Miles' domain. For MacElvey himself, however, Ernie had a cautious respect he seldom accorded counterjumpers. Mac was young, perhaps thirty, always carefully dressed, almost frail, but there was a sardonic tinge to his speech and in his lean face and green eyes that Ernie was wary of. Eight months ago MacElvey had stepped off a westbound stage, a tired-looking man with a dry and constant cough. He'd asked Miles for a job as clerk. After Miles bought out McKeogh, Mac had taken over the management of the store and was keeping Rainbow's books too. Truscott, at the bank, wanted him, but MacElvey was content here because Miles, knowing a good manager when he saw one, paid him more than Truscott could.

"Where's the boss, Mac?" Ernie greeted him.

MacElvey looked up. He was in shirt sleeves, but his vest was neatly buttoned, his cuffs rolled midway up his lean, freckled forearms. He glanced at Ernie and said dryly, "Looking for you."

"Anything special?"

MacElvey rose and took his coat from the back of the chair and shrugged it on, saying, "Ever hear of a man named Danning?"

"No."

"He's that drifter you stopped last night." He looked

at Ernie, his eyes gently mocking, and Ernie felt a pre-monition of trouble. Mac told him what had happened this morning, and a slow wrath stirred in Ernie.

"If I'd known that, I'd have herded him back to town. I just passed him on the south road, heading out of the country."

"Heading for Box H," MacElvey corrected dryly. "Della Harms took him on."

Ernie straightened up and said, "Where's Younger?"

"With O'Hea. O'Hea saw it, too. Miles wants us, so come along."

"O'Hea," Ernie said grimly, a bottomless contempt in the word.

They left the store, heading upstreet and turning right at Melaven's saloon. Several people on the street spoke to MacElvey who returned their greetings courteously but unsmilingly. Beyond Bell's barbershop there was a gap in the boardwalk for the drive through the high board fence into Shufeldt's lumberyard, and beyond was the Masonic Hall, a two-story frame building whose upper floor was the town's social center. The ground floor, with a center entrance between two big windows, like most of the stores in town, was the Hardison County Courthouse. It was the monument to the dislike of a county only one genera-tion old for the necessities of law.

The first door down the corridor on the left was nailed shut; the second opened onto a small waiting room which held a half-dozen wired barrel chairs. The yellowed calendar illustrations on the wall, the cold stove in its sandbox, the flyblown single window, unwashed in years, reminded most callers on official business of a hostler's cubbyhole in a livery stable.

Ernie, leading the way, walked through this room toward the door in the front wall, which was closed. He didn't knock, but opened the door and stepped in, and MacElvey followed him, closing the door behind him.

This was a large room, and what would ordinarily have been the show window was painted an opaque white more than half its height. This formed the front wall of the office, and to its right against the wall was an ancient rolltop desk. Sheriff O'Hea sat in the swivel chair before it, his feet cocked up on the lower drawer of the desk, which he had pulled out for a footrest. He looked over his shoulder at Ernie and MacElvey, and his sallow, jowly face with its watery blue eyes—the face of a sick and unhappy spaniel— did not alter its expression.

Ernie didn't even look at him. His glance settled on Younger Miles, who was half seated on the table pushed against the closed corridor door.

Miles said, "You meet him, Ernie?" and Ernie replied grimly, "Yeah, I didn't know," and moved over to one of the three chairs against the back wall. He put his legs out straight and shoved his hat off his forehead, waiting.

Mac put his shoulder against the wall by the door and said nothing.

Younger came to his feet and rammed his hands in

his hip pockets and came over to O'Hea. Hatless now, so that his fine light hair, short and curly, disclosed the blocky shape of his head, he seemed a young man striving for the solidity and drabness of middle-age prosperity. His suit was dark, well cut, his boots gleaming, but he could no more have hidden his strength and alertness than a little girl can hide her age by dressing in her mother's clothes. His chest was deep, his back wide and massive, and his hands had the wide meaty spread at the palms of a man who has labored with his full strength. His mustache did not fully hide his straight mouth, and his hooded eyes, as he paused and looked down at O'Hea now, were bright and searching and black as tar, with the shiny opaque surface of tar too. His face, browned from the sun, held a spot of color at each heavy cheekbone.

"Let's see those dodgers," he demanded.

Sheriff O'Hea pulled out two lower drawers of his desk and tiredly lugged them across the room and dumped the contents on the table, which was already cluttered with ore samples, newspapers, boxes of cartridges and miscellaneous gear.

Younger followed him, and Ernie, watching a moment, said, "You figure he's wanted?"

Younger turned to him. "If we can find a reward dodger that fits him, we can claim he is."

"Then what?" Ernie said, scoffing mildly.

"Load him on a stage and ship him out of the country, then turn him loose. He'll drift."

Ernie yawned, and then said idly, "Hell, there's one

way to deal with a saloon bum like that. Rough him up. Give me Stew and Bill Arnold to stand off that Henhouse crew and I'll break a singletree over him. Let him crawl out of the country after that."

"That's just what I don't want," Miles said coldly. "This'll be legal and respectable, nothing rough. He insulted Mrs. Miles. It could have been any other woman. We push him out of the country, and we're rid of him. Rainbow hasn't showed in it, and it's all quiet."

MacElvey said dryly, "Maybe it's quiet."

Younger shifted his glance to him. "Why won't it be, Mac?"

Mac said, "He looks to me like the kind that wouldn't go anywhere unless he wanted to. Maybe he won't want to go."

Younger regarded him thoughtfully, as if he were giving his statement respectful consideration. "What would you do, Mac?"

"Ignore him."

Younger smiled faintly, without humor. "Hell, I'm going to get Henhouse, Mac. I'm going to move in on everything those two women haven't got title to, and then I'll buy 'em out. All legal. And I don't want a nosy, sorehead puncher stirring them up to fighting. No. He goes."

"Listen to this," O'Hea interrupted, and he quoted: "'About six feet tall, weighs one seventy, age about 30. Dark complexion, surly appearance, light gray eyes, black hair. This man is quarrelsome and dangerous, armed or unarmed. Wanted for horse stealing and brand changing by the Jackson County authorities.'" He looked at Miles. "That close enough?"

"For Mrs. Harms and Della, yes," Miles said dryly. "Arrest him and put him on the Petrie stage tonight and dump him over the mountains, O'Hea."

Ernie said jibingly, "O'Hea and who else?"

The three of them regarded O'Hea now, and he glanced at Ernie with a quiet hatred and moved back to his chair. He sat down with the slowness of a sick man who knows he will move slowly until he dies. He said, not looking at Miles, "I'd like help."

"I bet you would," Ernie scoffed.

"Quit it, Ernie," Younger said absently. He scrubbed his face with the palm of his heavy hand frowning, and then he looked at MacElvey.

"Mac, you work for me, but they like you around here, and you're a steady head. They'll figure O'Hea's doing it the quiet way. He's entitled to a deputy. What about it?"

"You pay me," Mac said laconically.

Miles looked at him closely, and MacElvey returned his stare evenly, his green eyes unblinking. Miles turned away then and said, "Then you and Ernie get the horses."

MacElvey and Ernie rose and went out, and O'Hea began the slow process of putting the dodgers back in the drawers. He replaced the drawers then and sank wearily again into the chair.

Miles, standing in the middle of the room, moodily

lighted a cigar, and when he had it going well, he reached for his hat on the table.

"Make it stick," he said briefly to O'Hea.

O'Hea poked at some papers on his desk, looking sidewise at them, and said without looking up, "Got a minute, Younger?"

Miles had his hat on. He paused in the middle of the room and said "Sure."

O'Hea said, still jabbing gently at the papers, "Ever stop to think this wouldn't have happened if Abbie hadn't been drinking?"

"I've thought about it," Younger said coldly. "Have you?"

O'Hea looked at him now, a faint surprise in his face. "She's your wife."

"You raised her. I picked her up when she was baking pies for a living at the hotel and hadn't had a new dress in three years. What's the matter? Is good food, all the money she wants, a new home and the respect of the country a little too strong for the O'Hea blood?"

"That's what I'm gettin' at," O'Hea said doggedly. "What's the matter with her?"

"She's trash," Miles said brutally, and he watched the color mount in O'Hea's cheeks. A faint anger stirred in O'Hea's eyes and faded slowly, and Younger went on, no mercy in his voice, "I don't give a damn what happens to her, O'Hea, just so she doesn't drag my name into the muck. Because, by Heaven, I'm going to be respected. I married her and gave her a home. I bought a bunch of cows for you and run them on shares with mine, free. All I ask for pay is that she keeps out of the gutters and you go through the motions of bein' a sheriff. That's asking a lot, it looks like."

O'Hea said nothing, and Miles went to the door and paused, his hand on the knob.

"Just hold on a little longer, O'Hea. I'll be big enough to name my own sheriff in a year or two. And by God, I won't have to marry his daughter, either." He went out.

O'Hea ceased playing with the papers now and stared somberly at his hand. He noted, with a sick bitterness, that it was old and veined and trembling. He clenched his fist slowly, and then with more strength, and then more, until his lips were drawn across his teeth with the violence of his effort. Then he unclenched his hand and looked at it. The fingers still trembled. Presently, his glance lifted to the window and his eyes were dead, without hope, resigned.

Chapter V

The Box H stood just away from the foothills where they leveled off onto the Blackbow Flats, and lay at the foot of long sloping bald hills. It was a small, well weathered place, built of logs, square and practical, its few trees big and startling on the bare face of the flats. The outbuildings were modest, too, and Danning, looking at the place in the bright morning sun, could almost guess its history. Harms had probably come out here with a young wife and baby looking for poor man's grass. He'd homesteaded here on the Flats, thrown up a crude sod shack to get his family out of the weather, and then borrowed to the limit on cattle he could graze in the mountains. This, then, was the place he had finally built, the first triumph of a stubborn man, and, Danning thought, it might have been the way he would have started.

They came off the bald hill into the shaded yard. A massive cottonwood cast a wide pool of black shadow behind the house, and Della pulled under it and reined in the team. Against the sunny side of the house was a pretty bed of flowers and Chris noted the curtains in the windows. Only this, and the absence of men's gear in the yard, gave it a touch of the feminine.

There was a long slanting lean-to on the rear of the house, and a woman stepped out the door of it and came out to meet them. Mrs. Harms was a grave-faced woman of fifty, straight, inches shorter than Della, with a kind of stern optimism in her eyes. She wore a gay apron, and Danning saw her hands were rough, capable and work-worn.

"Mother, this is our new foreman, Chris Danning," Della said.

A faint surprise showed in Mrs. Harms' face in spite of herself, but her gaze never faltered from Chris' face.

He stepped out of the saddle and took off his hat, and accepted Mrs. Harms' warm, hard hand.

61

"I'm glad you're here, Mr. Danning. We've needed you."

Chris said, "Thank you, Mrs. Harms."

Della said, "Chris, if you'll dump that sack of groceries on the porch, I'll show you where to unhitch. The crew is scattered this morning."

Chris shouldered the sack of groceries out of the buckboard and tramped over to the lean-to door.

When he was out of earshot, Mrs. Harms looked up at her daughter, and for a moment they regarded each other in silence.

"Since when did we start hiring men of that stripe, Della?" Mrs. Harms asked calmly.

Della answered promptly, without smiling, "Since we acquired Younger Miles for a neighbor, mother." She paused. "What's wrong with him?"

Mrs. Harms didn't have time to answer before Chris returned. Della drove on to the wagon shed, passing the small log bunkhouse on the way. She showed Chris where to put the buckboard and hang the harness, and then told him to come in for dinner when he was finished, and left him.

Chris watched her walk away from him, striding purposefully toward the house, and he guessed she would have much to explain to her mother. For Chris sensed that Della had come to as sudden and reckless a decision this morning as he had, and that it was a momentous one for her.

He unhitched the team and turned them into the corral and noticed, now, the Box H brand on one of the horses.

It was a large square with the letter H inside, and with only a little imagination it could seem like a square-fronted shed with the door in the middle. It was plain enough why it had come to be called Henhouse.

He unsaddled his own travel-leaned sorrel gelding and his pack horse, and turned them in the corral and then paused a moment to look at the layout around him.

One thing was answered for him immediately. The crew wasn't slipshod. The place was in repair, the fences good, the corrals clean, the gear stowed out of the weather and everything under roof that should be. He wondered idly what these three men he would boss were like. He tramped over to his bedroll and hoisted it to his shoulder, and went on toward the bunkhouse.

It was built of small logs, and was the least weathered of the ranch buildings. He stepped into the open door, and then came to a halt and looked about him. Here, he saw in an instant, was his answer to the kind of crew Box H employed.

For the room was neat as a military barracks. Three of the six bunks against the back wall held blankets, and these blankets were made up. Clothes hung neatly from nails in the wall, and the board floor was swept and had lately been scrubbed. The tattered magazines on the big table in the center of the room were stacked in trim piles, and the barrel stove in the front corner was polished blackly. He crossed the room and dumped his bedroll and warbag in one of the top bunks and then went over to the overhead kerosene lamp above the table. He pulled it down and looked, and then hoisted it back in place again. Yes, even the lamp chimney was clean.

He stood motionless a moment, measuring this evidence and not liking it. He hadn't seen these men yet, but he knew them already, for this bunkhouse, home to three men, was clean, neat, swept up, picked up; it argued that its tenants were settled and satisfied and comfortable—and soft. He could guess their ages at between thirty and fifty-five, three men who had found haven in this quiet job where they were fed and paid well by two women, and where they paid back these kindnesses by painting buggies or building cupboards or transplanting flowers. He thought meagerly, *I won't get help here. I'd better kill him and then get out,* and for a moment he stood hesitant.

The clang of the dinner iron moved him at last. He washed at the bench and bucket outside the door and tramped across to the lean-to, entered, and seated himself at the big table there. After the custom of the country, he turned over his plate, helped himself to the food and began eating. The clean, flowered oilcloth and the matched china plates and cups he noted, and he felt an indefinable irritation at sight of them.

Presently Mrs. Harms came out, took the seat next him nearest the kitchen and Della sat down across from him. He ate steadily and silently, taking no part in their conversation, not even hearing it, and when he was finished he excused himself, about to rise, when Mrs.

Harms said, "Smoke here, Chris. All the boys do."

Chris patiently rolled and lighted a slim cigarette, knowing Mrs. Harms wanted to quiz him and knowing, too, that this was the price he must pay for a kind of security. He could tell that Della was worried about her mother approving him, but that it wasn't going to change her plans.

Mrs. Harms started it by saying, "Have you worked around this country, Chris?"

He moved his dark head in negation. "No, Ma'm. I put in six years as trail boss for a drovers' outfit in Texas. Three years at Hashknife—Texas, too. I worked around before that, mostly in dry country."

"Have you ever run an outfit before as big as this?"

"If you run more than three thousand head, I haven't, Ma'm."

A faint smile touched Della's lips, but she did not look up.

Mrs. Harms persisted. "I'd think with your experience, you'd own your own place."

A wicked flicker of anger mounted in Chris' eyes and died, and he did not answer.

Della looked at him pleadingly, as if trying to tell him to have patience, as Mrs. Harms moved her plate aside and put both elbows on the table.

She said now, "I suppose Della's told you why we hired you."

Della put down her fork and, looking at Chris, said, "He's here to fight Younger Miles, mother. He understands that."

"You shouldn't say that, Della," Mrs. Harms said quietly. "It's just that— Well, it never hurts to carry a big stick."

"Chris is here, mother, to keep what we've got and get back what's ours. Let's not pretend," Della said firmly.

Mrs. Harms shook her head. "You make it sound as if we've gone out of our way to hunt trouble."

Chris said quietly, "You have, Mrs. Harms. If Della hasn't told you that, she should. I'm trouble. And she asked me to come. I didn't ask her."

She looked at him for a long moment, and his gray gaze didn't falter. It was Mrs. Harms who looked away first, and there was a quiet despair in her eyes. She rose and went into the house and Della, watching her, half started out of her chair and then settled back. There was a stubbornness in her face now as she went on eating, and Chris thought grimly, *She won't like any of it, Della.*

A pair of riders passed under the big cottonwood and Della looked out and saw them and called, "Mother, Leach and Andy are in."

There was no answer. Chris excused himself the second time, and now Della rose with him. "Come out and meet them," she said.

As they stepped out of the lean-to into the sun and headed for the corral, Della's face was somber, and Chris knew she was thinking of her mother and of the decision her mother couldn't face.

Presently she said gently, "Chris, there's just one

thing you've got to promise in all this. I'll take your word for it."

Chris waited, wondering what this new condition would be.

"That you'll finish this with Rainbow. I don't know why you hate Younger Miles, and I don't care. And I don't care what it costs us, but, in the end, you've got to leave us safe."

Chris was silent a few steps, pondering this, and then he said, "I'll promise that," and made his condition. "If you move your mother to town, Della, I'll promise it."

Della looked swiftly up at him, something like fright in her eyes, and did not answer.

The two riders had turned their horses into the corral and were coming toward the house. The smaller man was the older, and Chris didn't even look at him but watched the tall man with the big hands. As they came closer, Chris' hopes suddenly died. The big man was in his middle thirties and wore clean, wash-faded levis and calico shirt. He had an open, simple face, and nothing showed in it except the placidity of a drudge. Chris had seen his kind, the hired man of the Kansas homesteads who plows another man's fields for thirty years in order to get a field of his own where he dies, questioning nothing.

The other man was different, and when they halted before Della, it was this first man she introduced first.

"Chris, this is Leach Conover. And Andy West. Boys, this is Chris Danning, our new foreman."

Leach put out his hand, but it was done reluctantly, and an immediate hostility crept into his eyes. His browned face under his high-crowned Stetson was old with the lines of defeat and forgotten bitterness. *A tired old dog lying in the sun,* Chris thought without pity, for he knew Leach liked his life and himself the way they were, comfortable and forgotten.

Andy West said, as he shook hands, "You're workin' for a wonderful boss, Mr. Danning."

"Yes," Chris said.

Leach was eyeing Della almost with accusation but she did not see it.

She said to Chris, "I'll help mother, and then we'll talk, Chris."

They left him, and he cut slowly over to the bunkhouse. *The Henhouse,* he thought quietly. It was a good name, perhaps, with Della the reluctant mother hen. Yet somewhere here there must be some iron in somebody besides Della. The two men he'd met would shun responsibility instinctively and, if given it, would drift. There was a third man, then. Perhaps he would be what Chris wanted and had to have, but Chris expected nothing.

Inside the bunkhouse, he looked about him again and chose his bunk, the top one closest the door. He dumped out the contents of his warbag on the floor and hung his few clothes on a vacant nail, and then unlashed his bedroll.

As he worked, he heard a rider pass, and supposed it was Leach or Andy. He was picking up a pair of boots

68

from the remaining gear on the floor when he heard a man enter the room behind him and, boots in hand, he turned.

The man hauled up at sight of him, and they looked at each other a long moment. Recognition came to them both at the same time.

"You stopped me this mornin'," the man said. "There at Melaven's, you told me about Mrs. Miles."

"That's right," Chris said. This, then, was the third man of the Box H crew. A kind of sardonic amusement rose in Chris then as he remembered his hopes, and he silently chucked his boots in the bunk.

The third Box H hand, Frank Yordy, had a bluff, self-important manner about him that could never, Chris thought bitterly, deceive even a child. He was heavy, but with soft flesh hanging on his bones, and he had the ruddy complexion, the challenging eye and the bold voice of a man who has discovered he can live by his mouth and nothing much else. He was the sort who knew all the saloon gossip and was full of vast schemes and hard luck stories, and who charmed women of all ages with his calculated gallantries.

Yordy, standing just inside the door now, watched him as he picked up a worn jumper and fumbled in its pockets.

"What're you doin' in this place?" Yordy demanded then.

"I work here."

For a full ten seconds Yordy was silent. Chris finally looked up and surprised the expression of amazement just fading from Yordy's florid face.

"Not after this morning, you ain't," Yordy announced.

Chris didn't say anything. He went on sorting out his gear.

Yordy came into the room, put a hand against the wall and crossed his feet. He shook his head pityingly and said, "You don't have the sense God gave you, fella, after what you did this morning. If you had, you'd be clean over the Blackbows right now. We don't take your kind of talk in this country."

Still Chris didn't say anything, and Yordy came erect. "You'll be out of here in ten minutes, soon's Mrs. Harms knows about this morning."

He turned and went out and, unsmilingly, Chris watched him go. Here was the Box H crew, the men Della promised would back him up. A clumsy, slow-witted hand fit only to break horses, a burnt-out and bitter old man who wanted only to sit by the stove each night, and a blustering fool. Two were useless, the third dangerous, and he was expected to beat Rainbow with them.

He went to the door and watched Yordy swagger importantly toward the house, and he thought with a gray disgust, *He'll have to go.* He'd made a bad bargain, and he'd worsened it by promising Della to finish it with Rainbow, so Box H would be safe. Yordy, though, was too much. *I'll drift,* he thought suddenly. *Miles won't do anything more to her now, if I leave, than if I hadn't been here.*

About to turn, a movement atop the low, bald hill

70

where the road came down caught his eye. He waited, then, until he made out two horsemen, and curiosity held him still in the doorway until he recognized Sheriff O'Hea and the red-headed man in Miles' store as they reined up under the cottonwood.

A slow suspicion held him motionless as he watched them dismount and meet Della, who came out of the lean-to. Moments later, Yordy came out, too, then West and Conover and finally Mrs. Harms. Presently, he saw Della turn to look at the bunkhouse, and Yordy gestured sweepingly toward it.

A kind of cross-grained pride held Chris there while Della fell in beside O'Hea and walked with him toward the bunkhouse. The others, all save Mrs. Harms, dropped in behind them.

Chris stood full in the doorway, hands at his sides, as Della and O'Hea halted before him.

Della had a piece of folded paper in her hand. She said in quiet distress, "Chris, Sheriff O'Hea wants to talk to you."

Chris looked at O'Hea.

"Have you ever been in Jackson County, Wyoming?" O'Hea asked.

Chris looked from him to MacElvey, whose expression was one of sardonic watchfulness.

"I have," Chris said.

"Then I guess that settles it, son," O'Hea went on, a kind of thin and forced authority in his voice. "They want you there, and I'll have to send you back."

"He means you're under arrest, Chris," Della said.

71

She looked at O'Hea. "Don't you tell him what for?"

"Brand changing," O'Hea said.

"He's a horse thief," Yordy said bluntly. "No drifter ever bought a horse like he turned into the corral, not on chuckline handouts."

"You don't know that, Frank!" Della said sharply. She turned to Chris and held out the paper, which Chris now saw was a dodger. "Do you want to read it?"

Chris only shook his head in negation. "Do you believe it?" he asked her.

"I—" she looked searchingly at him. "I would hate to."

"And you still want me for a foreman?"

"Yes, if this isn't true."

Chris lifted his gaze directly to MacElvey, watched him a moment and then said quietly to him alone, "Don't get in this." His gaze now shifted to Yordy, standing next O'Hea.

"You," he said flatly to Yordy, "saddle up and clear out of here. We'll leave your stuff at the hotel. Only get out of here. Now."

An expression of blank and furious amazement crept into Yordy's heavy face. He glanced quickly at Della, who was not looking at him, and then at O'Hea, who was watching Chris, and only afterwards did he look at Chris. He had calculated the risk and accepted it, and said flatly, "Not when any horse thief tells me, foreman or not."

Chris stepped out of the bunkhouse, not fast, took the three steps to Yordy and with his left hand fisted a wad of Yordy's shirt for purchase. He pulled Yordy toward him and slapped him once across the mouth with the flat of his hand. His blow carried his hand past Yordy's head, and he brought it back, slapping Yordy again with the back of his hand. He slapped him a third time, then, deliberately, and let his hands fall to his sides waiting.

Yordy hesitated long past the surprise of it, and then, crowded by pride and fear, hit him. The rest of it was violent, utterly silent, so brief there was no time for those watching it to move. Chris hit him in the belly, and when Yordy jack-knifed, Chris' shoulder, low and lifting, caught him under the chin. As Yordy straightened, head back, Chris chopped in a blow from the side that almost swiveled Yordy's head on his neck. Yordy went down, not on his back, but like a man dropped, without volition and without struggle. He lay against Chris' shins for a moment, and then pushed himself to his knees. On all fours, he shook his head slowly three times, and then lurched to his feet, and without looking at them, he walked uncertainly in the direction of the corral.

Chris half turned now and looked at O'Hea, and his face was still hard with stirring anger.

"If you want to take me out of here, sheriff, try it," he invited.

The transition was too sudden for O'Hea; he was still looking at Yordy, so that when he caught the sound of Chris' voice and shifted his glance to him, the astonishment was still in his tired face.

73

In the long moment of silence that followed, with them all looking at him, O'Hea's expression changed slowly to a fleeting anger which was now only the dregs of an old courage, and then the tired defeat was there again. He seemed to gather up his pride and all his authority as he said, without moving, "Put a gun on him, Mac."

"If you do, you better use it, Red," Chris said to MacElvey.

"After you, O'Hea," MacElvey said dryly.

Nobody spoke or moved and, when Chris had given O'Hea his chance and it had not been accepted, he said with a brutal directness, "Get Miles off your back, O'Hea, or quit. Tell Miles to work it rough and in the open from now on. He knows how."

He looked at MacElvey, since this was for him, too, and he saw that MacElvey was watching him with strange speculation in his green eyes.

O'Hea tried to put a kind of dignity in his words now, and a threat too. "You won't come?"

"No."

O'Hea said to Della, "I think we'd better have a talk, Della," and he tramped past Chris toward the house. MacElvey fell in beside Della, who gave Chris a frightened sober glance as she passed him.

That left Leach and Andy with him, and Chris regarded them with a quiet irony in his gray eyes. "You don't like it, Andy," he said dryly, his words a statement, not a question.

Andy West's still-puzzled face altered now. He

74

flushed, reading the jibe rightly, but his answer reached far behind his disapproval and surprised Chris. "Was he right? You on the dodge?"

"No."

Andy's slow mind turned this over, balancing all that he had seen and understanding only now the implications.

Chris helped him. "The door's still open. Walk out if you want, or stay and fight Rainbow."

Andy nodded almost to himself. "I ain't ever shot at a man."

Chris didn't say anything, but looked at Leach. Yordy was riding past now. He looked neither to right nor left of him, but held stubbornly to the wagon tracks and walked his horse.

Leach watched Yordy a long moment, and then met Chris' gaze. "I been in trouble," he said meagerly. "I don't like it."

"Want your time?"

"Did I ask for it?" Leach demanded.

Chris moved his head in negation, acknowledging Leach's way of accepting this, and said then, sealing it, "I want to ride boundary tomorrow. Who shows it to me—Della?"

Leach and Andy looked at each other, and it was Andy who made the decision. "I do, I reckon," he said quietly.

Chapter VI

Frank Yordy didn't even look back at the place he'd worked these five years as he topped the bald hill above Box H. He spurred his horse impatiently, but soon, alone now and with the bright silence of midday around him, he relaxed and rolled a cigarette. The process of building his smoke took some concentration, since the hand he'd hit Danning with was sore and stiff already, and he thought of it with a small pride. He'd hit him, anyway. He wondered morosely why Danning had been standing there, no guard on him, when he'd ridden out, and he figured O'Hea had made a mistake.

Once his cigarette was lighted, he pasted it in the corner of his loose, sullen mouth and took stock of his situation. He knew now where he'd made his mistake. If he'd taken Della's orders to accept Danning as the new foreman instead of arguing with her, he'd be all right now. So he was out of a job now, an easy job that had given him good food, pleasant society, just the right amount of work, influence over two women and the complete domination of two men. The anger, this time at his own black luck, came back to him again, and he thought of Danning and the Harms women with a hot and bitter hatred.

The tawny flats lay on all sides of him, deceptively level in the overhead sun that cast no shadow. Yordy looked at the range now with the eye of a man who has, in the past, worried about its condition. It had been a dry summer, and this grass would barely keep fat on a range cow through the winter. Yordy thought of the bunch of two-year-olds that Della was going to have to buy feed for this winter, and the thought pleased him now, whereas this morning it had been worrying him. Why did he care? Henhouse's hard luck was his good luck, he thought now.

An hour later he came to the bridge over Coroner Creek, and put his horse down for a drink, watching the clear water brawling over the rocky bottom. He went on and was presently near the juncture of the Coroner Canyon road that ran string-straight from Triumph to the Blackbows and over the pass. Approaching it, he saw a rider coming from the mountains, and he raised his hand and felt his jaw; it was swollen, but not much. A sudden surge of bravado came to him. To hell with what anyone thought. He'd taken a licking from Danning while trying to save Della Harms from a criminally foolish move. Yordy had already begun to taste the pleasures of martyrdom.

As he drew closer to the crossroads, he saw that the rider was Mrs. Miles. A nice instinct for comfortable survival told Yordy that if he could make his story pitiful enough, he might, through Mrs. Miles' intercession, be taken on at Rainbow. Beyond that, however, was the woman herself, pretty, friendly, but an object of sly gossip and curiosity among the riffraff

Yordy liked. And a drinker, according to this gossip.

Yordy reached the crossroads first and reined up, and when Abbie Miles approached, he touched his hat respectfully and said, "Nice day, Mrs. Miles," and put his horse beside hers.

"Beautiful," Abbie agreed pleasantly. "Almost too nice, Frank. Is your range burning out like everyone else's?" Abbie rode her big chestnut sidesaddle. She wore a suit of some dark green material with divided skirt, and a tricorn hat that did not begin to pen her rich, raven hair. There was something almost shy about her greeting, and Yordy, remembering Danning's disclosure, and wise in the ways of many excesses, almost smiled. Remorse was making her humble, more pleasant than usual, even.

He kept his face grave, however, and shook his head slowly. "I haven't any interest in Box H range any more, Mrs. Miles. I'd say it was burning out, though."

Abbie looked closely at him, her blue eyes at once full of concern. "You mean you've left, Frank."

"I was thrown off," Yordy said calmly, with just the right tinge of sadness in his tone. He glanced over at Mrs. Miles and saw that his news was having the desired effect, for she was troubled.

"That would take a pretty good man, Frank."

"He is a pretty good man. Or at least the Harms women think so, because that's why they hired him."

"Who is he?" Abbie asked curiously.

"Chris Danning, a drifter," Frank said, watching Abbie. But the name seemed not to register, and Yordy

78

thought with an amused malice, *She don't even know who brought her home.*

"And what's he doing there?"

"Gettin' ready to tie into Rainbow," Frank said bluntly. "I guess it's no news to you, Mrs. Miles, that there's bad blood between Rainbow and Box H."

"No," Abbie said softly, not looking at him.

"I done my best to keep the peace," Yordy said gravely. "For my pains, I get pitched out by a stranger. Not even given time enough to get my clothes."

Abbie didn't say anything, and Frank sighed. "Well, there's other jobs. I'm not a young man any more, but I reckon I can find a place where my experience will mean something."

"I expect you can," Abbie said, and beyond that she was silent. Yordy glanced at her. She was looking out over the flats, and he wasn't at all sure she was listening. Even if she had heard him, she wasn't interested enough to help, and a wave of self-pity engulfed Yordy then that he nursed in silence until they were in sight of town.

His scheming, though, was tireless and thorough, and presently he spoke again, this time more directly. "I figure Younger could use some things I know, Mrs. Miles. That is, if he's serious about what he's doin' to Henhouse."

Abbie looked at him now, and there was a faint dislike in her eyes. "Things you'd be willing to sell, Frank?"

Yordy ignored that. "Henhouse can be licked, Dan-

79

ning or no Danning, and I know how." He looked fully at her. "You think he'd be interested?"

"Ask him, why don't you?"

They were in Triumph's main street now and when they'd passed the feed stable, Abbie pulled in at the hotel.

Frank reined up and touched his hat, and said in a low voice. "I'll be at Joe Briggs' for three-four days. You tell Younger that, will you?"

Abbie said, "Danning must be a big man, Frank, if he drives you to talk to my husband out at Briggs'."

Yordy's anger was immediate. His florid face darkened a little and he looked down at Abbie who did not trouble to hide her contempt now.

"You ought to know, Mrs. Miles," he said pointedly. "Good day to you."

Abbie watched him ride off, a faint puzzlement in her face. The old dread crept back then as she turned to halter her horse to the tie rail. Why ought she to know anything about Danning? The answer came, even as she asked herself the question. It had something to do with yesterday, with those hours that were dropped completely out of her life and which she could never account for. She couldn't pretend she remembered: Mrs. Flynn told her Ray Flanders had carried her in last night.

Abbie squared her shoulders, took a deep breath, ducked under the tie rail and stepped into the lobby of the hotel. It was deserted, but Abbie knew the routine of the place.

She went on through the dining room into the kitchen. On the way, she took off her hat and laid it on one of the dining-room tables and was rolling up her sleeves as she shouldered open the kitchen door.

Kate was working in the pantry at the big table under the open window that looked out onto the street. She was kneading bread in a great dishpan, the bread pans spread out on the table. Her sleeves were rolled and her arms floured to the elbows.

"Hello, handsome," Abbie greeted her, and went over to an apron hanging on a hook on the wall. "What's it tonight? Pie and cake, but what color of each?"

Kate smiled slowly. "Abbie, you're just like a ranch dog. Every time the door's open, you sneak in and head for the stove."

"I never get a chance at home," Abbie said calmly. "It's Mrs. Flynn's kitchen, not mine. If I can't work here, I'll forget how."

Abbie moved about the kitchen, talking cheerfully. She knew where everything was, since she was doing just this when Younger Miles had found her. She got the canned fruit, the pans and all the paraphernalia organized on the big table beside Kate, and then set to work. There was an utter contentment on her face as she busied herself now, but she was wondering, behind her chatter, how she was going to ask the questions she must have answered.

Presently she observed to Kate that she had ridden in with Yordy, and gave Yordy's account of what had happened at Box H.

Kate stopped kneading the bread a moment and listened, and there was an almost rapt expression in her small face as Abbie talked on.

"So he's started," Kate said quietly, when Abbie was finished. "Poor Della."

"When I told Yordy that Danning must be a pretty big man, Yordy said 'You ought to know, Mrs. Miles.'" She looked over at Kate. "Why should I, Kate?" She paused and said doggedly, "Yesterday?"

Kate nodded. "He took you home—part way home, that is. Ernie Coombs and some of your crew met him. They almost had a fight, since Ernie thought he was the one who'd got you drunk."

Abbie murmured sardonically, "What touching loyalty," and went back to her work. So did Kate, and presently, Abbie said, "Well, finish it, Katie."

"Not any more," Kate said quietly. "I've talked enough. There's a man around here, though, that I'd like to kill," she added grimly.

Abbie looked startled. "Who?"

"The man who's getting you that liquor."

The two women looked warily at each other and Abbie shrugged. "Let's not talk about it, Katie."

"Let's do!" Kate said hotly. "Your friends can cover up for you only so long, Abbie, and then something happens like this morning!"

"Something like what?"

There was real distress in Kate's face now, but she went on stubbornly, looking Abbie full in the face. "I guess Ernie and Younger wanted to make sure Danning didn't talk about you, so they gave him his choice of working for Rainbow or leaving the country. So Danning stood right in front of Melaven's this morning and announced to the whole town that he'd taken you home drunk last night, and what was Younger going to do about it? That's all that happened!"

The color drained out of Abbie's face as Kate finished, and she looked down at her hands. After a long moment she said, "Your Danning is a gentleman, isn't he?"

"My Abbie is a lady, too, isn't she?" Kate countered hotly. As soon as she'd said it, she was sorry. Tears started down Abbie's cheeks, and Kate folded her to her and held her and said miserably, "I'm sorry, darling. I'm a fool and a mean person, I guess."

Abbie sobbed brokenly, hiding her face in Kate's shoulder. "I—don't mind, really, Katie. Only—I'm so damned unhappy."

"I know you are."

"He doesn't *care* if I drink!" Abbie said with a soft wildness. "He doesn't care enough to wonder why, even."

"Move back here."

Abbie shivered. "He wouldn't let me. That's why he married me, to decorate the house and wear these clothes and ride those fine horses. That's what respectable people do, he says. Hasn't anyone ever told him respectable people love their wives, too?"

83

Kate said in a low, discouraged voice, "He's going to hurt you even more, Abbie. You've got to expect that."

"He couldn't," Abbie said miserably. She moved away from Kate now and wiped her eyes. "I guess he could too," she amended. "If he hurt Dad, that would be the end. I—I'd kill him."

"Be quiet, Abbie," Kate said miserably. She wiped the flour from her hands and then brushed off the flour dust that had come off on Abbie's dress, and as she did so she asked quietly, "What are you going to do when it gets worse? Drink more? Where does it end?"

Abbie looked steadily at her. "What does it matter where it ends, Kate? It hurts him a little. I wish it hurt him more. It hurts Dad, but that's his price for being kept. It hurts me and I don't care. Then what does it matter?"

"What about us, the ones who do love you?"

Abbie shook her head. "You've got to take me the way I am, Kate."

Abbie didn't reply further. She had no defense, and she wasn't going to try for one any longer. She turned stubbornly back to her work, and Kate, when she saw there was no use, turned back to hers. The two of them worked in silence, listening to the small street noises of late afternoon and the soft rush of the hot and waiting stove behind them.

Kate said, presently, "There's your father," and when Abbie looked out the window she saw O'Hea and MacElvey crossing over from the feed stable to

84

Miles' store. They parted there, O'Hea plodding tiredly, head on chest, up the boardwalk to the corner. At Melaven's he turned in. Abbie watched him silently, a deep pity stirring within her.

A moment later Perry MacElvey came out of the store and turned toward the corner too. He walked with a kind of alert and indolent grace, looking about him. His roving glance caught the open window in the hotel, and Kate waved to him. He touched his hat respectfully, and turned the corner.

Miles was boredly reading a paper at O'Hea's desk when he heard the footsteps in the corridor. He put down his paper and listened. A single set of footsteps, which meant it wasn't O'Hea and MacElvey. He shook out his paper again, but when the door opened he turned his head to look over his shoulder. It was MacElvey. Alone. Younger put down his paper, saying, "Where's Danning?"

"At the Box H," MacElvey said. While Younger, puzzled, watched him, MacElvey skidded one of the barrel chairs into the center of the room and leisurely seated himself.

A swift impatience at MacElvey came to Younger, and he demanded, "What happened out there? Where's O'Hea?"

"Danning laughed at us," MacElvey said. "He just wouldn't come. O'Hea's getting a drink he needs pretty badly."

Younger could not entirely keep the anger from his

voice as he said, "Start from the beginning!"

MacElvey told him the whole story, sparing none of the details. Younger interrupted him only once, when Mac told him of Danning daring O'Hea to take him.

"What did O'Hea do?"

"Told me to put a gun on him."

"And what did you do?"

"I didn't move a damned muscle," MacElvey answered evenly.

Younger came out of his chair and said in savage disgust, "Ah, hell, Mac!"

MacElvey said nothing, and there was no apology in his eyes. A wild temper was in Younger as he stood there watching him, and then MacElvey saw it fade. MacElvey said, "Do you know him, Younger?"

A hard, speculative caution came into Younger's dark eyes now. "Could I forget him if I did? Why?"

"He said you know how to make it rough. He sounded like he knew."

Younger only grunted, watching Mac. He stood utterly still a few seconds, as if thinking back, reaching, wondering, and then he said in a soft, wicked voice, "He just guessed. And he guessed right."

The slow tramp of footsteps sounded in the hall, and Younger raised his glance to the door. O'Hea came in then, nodding to them, and hung up his Stetson.

"Get your drink?" Younger asked mildly.

"Why, yes. I'm not feeling good." O'Hea, heading for his chair, would not meet Younger's eyes.

Younger let him sit down and then said, still mildly,

"That's right, you're not feeling good. So you're writing a letter to the commissioners asking for six months' sick leave."

Still O'Hea didn't look at him, and Younger went on with an implacable and mocking gentleness. "You've got money for a deputy, O'Hea. Appoint him. If he suits the commissioners, there won't be any special election necessary. And I'll pick a man who'll suit them."

"Who?" MacElvey asked.

"You."

MacElvey said dryly, "I didn't do so well today."

"You'll learn, because you'll get some practice. At least you can fight your way out of a bushel basket." He looked contemptuously at O'Hea, and then back to MacElvey. "I'm going to work it rough and in the open. Danning's first move will be to claim for Henhouse what they had a year ago. When he moves, we hit him—rough and in the open. We'll get him, legal and respectable."

Again he looked at O'Hea, who had put both arms on the chair as if he were making an effort to hold himself erect.

"If we have to go beyond that, Mac, we'll go. Then you resign and O'Hea comes back into office." He regarded MacElvey now. "All right?"

"You pay me," MacElvey said, for the second time that day, and he shrugged.

Younger swiveled his glance to O'Hea. "I pay you, too," he said bluntly. "Write your letter."

Chapter VII

Seated in his chair on the veranda roof in the warm night, Walt Hardison had heard the team and buckboard drive up to the hotel. He had heard the two people, a man and a woman, get out, but they had not spoken. He had heard the man wrestle the trunk out of the buckboard and make several trips to unload gear, but he still had no clue to the man's identity.

So when, minutes later, Chris Danning stepped out onto the veranda roof and quietly greeted him, Walt had half the answer to his question. The rest of it came a few moments later after Danning had rolled and lighted his cigarette and settled back in his chair.

"I brought Mrs. Harms in tonight."

"Expecting trouble?"

"That's what I wanted to ask you."

Walt said nothing, curious as to what this taciturn drifter would ask him. It came immediately.

"I want to find out from you what Box H claimed and used up to a year and a half ago."

Walt considered the implications of that question and then said dryly, "Maybe you better bring Della in too."

There was no answer, and Walt knew in the darkness that there was no answering smile either. It wasn't that the man was humorless; he was just in dead and competent earnest, he thought.

Walt said obligingly, "Roy Harms ran his stuff as far west as that feeder creek on the other side of Thessaly Canyon. East, he never went beyond the old logging road you can still see. South, up to the boulder fields at timber line. North, his homestead boundary on the flats, and another homestead he bought out."

"So the rest is open range?"

"Not exactly," Walt said. "Harvey Finch owned Rainbow before Miles. He was first in the country, and he bought a good chunk of the flats and mountains from the Indians, trading beef and powder and some-times whisky for land. Some of it he had title to, and some he didn't. He'd sell it or give it away, as the whim took him. And he sold that stretch I just outlined to Roy Harms."

"Then it belongs to the Harms women?"

"No, again. When the reservation was surveyed, the survey pulled the boundary clean back over the Black-bows. The Indians never owned the land, so Finch never owned it, so Harms couldn't have bought it from him. It's open range, on the books." He looked at Danning's dark form in the chair. "There's your joker, son. Some men would figure Harms paid his money and the land was his. But not Miles."

"No," Chris said. He stood up now, and said quietly, "Thanks, old-timer."

"What do you aim to do now?"

"Take it all back," Chris said quietly.

Walt smiled in the dark and looked up at the tall man beside him. He wished he had more light out here; he would have liked to see Danning's face when he said that, although he could picture it well enough. Dead serious, indifferent, casual even, but dead serious.

He said, "Not Thessaly Canyon. Tip Henry had homesteaded that place, and he's a Rainbow hand. He'll sleep there, and Miles will put on the improvements for him and buy it from him. It's nothin' but a Rainbow line camp, but legally it's a homestead. One move against Tip and you'll have a U. S. Marshal on your neck. But I don't reckon I have to tell you that."

"No," Chris said. "Thanks."

He tramped across the roof and was almost to the door when Hardison called, "Son, will you tell me something?" Danning halted, waiting. "What did Sam O'Hea want you for?"

"Brand changing."

"Fools," Hardison muttered. "Good night."

Danning stepped into the corridor, and Walt listened to the solid tramp of his feet, as distinctive, in Walt's ears, as the sound of his voice. He had a sudden unaccountable longing, wild and unreasonable, for the use of his legs for just one week—just long enough to ride with this man, and know him, and share his luck. And then he smiled wryly into the night. *I'm a fool,* he thought. *His luck is that he'll die.*

Kate Hardison was seated in one of the lobby chairs, and when Chris came off the last step, she rose and came toward him. There was a dislike in her pale brown eyes that seemed to be carried over from their last meeting.

90

He halted, and she said, "You've got a good start, haven't you? You've moved Mrs. Harms out of her home, made a fool of our law officers, tattled on Mrs. Miles and beat up the Box H foreman."

"Mrs. Harms talks too much," Chris said mildly.

"When do you move Della in, so you can use Box H for whatever you want?"

"For brand changing?" Chris suggested.

"No. I don't think that. I just think you're using women and jobs and men and even acquaintances for your own business. What is your business, by the way?"

"My own."

They regarded each other with open hostility now, and Kate finally said, "I think you're sick. I think you're sick with hating—maybe yourself. We have troubles here, but they're little troubles compared to the kind you're bringing us. Why don't you ride on through?"

"As soon as I'm finished," Chris said. "Good night."

He went out to the buckboard and turned the team and drove south, out of the last lights of the town. There was a gadfly quality about Kate Hardison that he was coming to dislike. Everything he had done so far had a solid place in his plan, yet this girl, as if she intuitively knew that his headlong wrecking of Younger Miles would hurt a lot of innocent people, had fought him. Not with anything but words and scorn, but both were sharp.

He felt a sudden restlessness now, and in the quiet

91

night he fell back upon the old fantasy that always soothed him. It was an old fantasy, gray and secret as his hopes, and it had been part of his loneliness for more than a year now, festering its way into his soul and feeding his hatred. It was this: in his imagination, he had married Bess, and he had made a life for them. On the nights which now numbered in the hundreds, when he was camped in solitude by lonely fires, he lived that day with her—in his imagination. He followed her through each day's small duties, not as a man away from his women-folk might speculate fondly on activities at home but with the hungry, painstaking attention of a man who has never known a home. He had imagined a continuing life for Bess and himself. In it, they had bought the small ranch they planned on, and he had ridden for the midwife that delivered his son, Ben. He had nursed Bess back to health and played with the boy, and they had ridden over every acre of their small holding. He had driven their first beef to the shipping point and had handed Bess the check. Always, in his accursed imagination, she was the most desirable of women, with a beautiful slow smile and the low, almost husky voice that drove his misery deeper and deeper. He would not let her die.

But tonight, it would not come right. Long before he reached the bald hill in front of the Box H, he had given it up, and the old waking restlessness was on him again. The stars were low and bright, and when he came down the grade the place was dark. The Dipper

92

told him it was two hours past midnight; he felt awake and impatient.

He turned the team into the corral, and his sorrel, close to the open pasture gate on the far side of the corral, drifted over to him. Three other horses who had left off their night feeding to trail in for water, followed the sorrel back into the corral, too.

Chris, stroking his gelding's neck, looked at the stars again and came to his decision. He circled the horses and closed the corral gate into the pasture, then tramped over to the dark bunkhouse.

He went to the bunk below his own and felt Andy sleeping with his face to the wall. Putting a hand on Andy's shoulder, he shook him, and when Andy turned over, Chris said in a low voice, "Let's start now."

Andy only mumbled, and Chris repeated, "Let's start now," remembering that Mrs. Harms' last act before she left for town in the evening was to silently disapprove of the few supplies Chris took from the kitchen in preparation for the boundary ride. They were on the table behind him.

Andy uncomplainingly rolled out, and Chris put the few supplies in his blankets and they silently left the bunkhouse without waking Leach.

In closing the pasture gates, Chris had trapped a second-string horse of Andy's which Andy cheerfully agreed to take.

They saddled and rode out into the still night, and Chris, thankful to be in the saddle again, rolled a cigarette and lighted it. He was debating where to start his survey, which he hoped would acquaint him with all of Box H range, new and old, when Andy spoke from beside him:

"You'll likely want a look at the Falls first, because that's where the best stuff is."

"The Falls?" Chris echoed.

"It's where Elder Creek drops into a canyon," Andy said. "A big box canyon about five miles long and belly deep with the sweetest grass a cow ever grazed in. The mouth is so narrow we put up a brush fence acrost it first thing this spring, figurin' to hold the feed for Della's prize hundred this fall. Ain't anything been in it, not even deer."

"And what are the prize hundred?" Chris asked, curious now.

"A hundred head of two-year-olds we're holdin' over and feedin' with a spoon almost," Andy said, a quiet pride in his voice. "They got two inches of tallow on 'em now. Last week we turned 'em into Falls Canyon, and by the first snow they'll be fat enough to roll down the flats. Miss Della's made arrangements to feed 'em through the winter and—"

"Bought feed?" Chris cut in.

"That's right," Andy said placidly. "Her and Yordy figured there wasn't grass enough on the flats to carry 'em through the winter after the dry summer. But they'll be prime stuff next summer."

Chris was silent a moment, considering this. "How far have we got to drive to a shipping point?"

"Hundred and forty miles south," Andy said.

Chris looked at him in the darkness but Andy was not aware of the look. A hundred and forty mile drive over the mountains to a railroad would run off all the tallow it had taken a year to put on, Chris knew. That was like Yordy, looking for the short cut to big money, gambling on a scheme basically unsound with Della's money to back it. Chris didn't know what arrangements Della had made for winter feed, but they must be canceled, the two-year-olds shipped this fall and the scheme to hold them over forgotten.

Andy, garrulous now, was patiently describing the extent and quality of the Box H range, but Chris was not listening. When Andy fell silent, Chris asked, "Is there a trail into Thessaly Canyon from the upper end? Not the lower end, the upper end."

Andy said reluctantly, "Yes." He waited a moment and said, "It ain't our range, though."

"Let's have a look," Chris said mildly. "I want to see that shack they're raising, but on the quiet."

"Now?"

"That's right."

Andy didn't comment, but his very silence contrived to express his distaste for this. After a short stretch of the flats, the country began to tilt to the first step of the foothills and they took to a trail now, Andy's horse in the lead.

They came out shortly onto a bench which, with its long, fingerlike mesas reaching out from the mountains, was the last of the open country.

The smell of pine timber was presently in the air and the clumps of cedar gave way to scattered black timber. The footfalls of their horses were quieter now on the soft humus of pine needles, and presently the stars overhead were blotted out by the pine forest. The smell of resin was all about them as they rode.

Chris could only judge the grade now by feeling how his horse worked; and when they paused to blow their horses in a clearing of the timber, he turned and looked back over the flats. He could see only the faintest dusting of lights at a point to the north and east which would be sleeping Triumph; the rest was a gray expanse below that faded gently into the black of the night sky.

They went on, still climbing, and presently crossed a creek and they clung to it for a while, still climbing, and after a bit Chris, spotting the Dipper again, said, "Andy, is this safe country for a fire? I don't want to make smoke in daylight."

Andy thought a moment and said slowly, "I reckon. Up a ways, though."

"Good. Let's light and eat."

Ten minutes up the trail, Andy pulled off the trail by the side of the stream. He built up a fire while Chris broke out the coffee pot and filled it in the stream and put it on the fire. Then Chris filled a frypan full of bacon and put it beside him. He squatted by the fire and rolled a smoke and Andy moved around the fire and knelt by it. He put his big hands to it as a man unconsciously does in front of a fire, be it summer or winter, and all his movements were slow and deliberate.

Chris looked curiously at him; his face was placid, content, and Chris wondered. He was reaching down into the flour sack for a cold biscuit to chew on when the shot came. The report of the rifle was flat, sharp, shattering the night stillness. It no sooner registered on Chris' hearing than the coffeepot went kiting off the fire, its spilled water hissing on the coals.

Andy's mouth opened. His hands were still turned to the fire, and he closed his mouth to speak and was rising uncertainly when Chris said quietly, "Don't move, Andy. He just wants to talk to us."

And he lazily threw Andy a biscuit which Andy caught by reflex. Only then did Chris look up the trail; he sat motionless, thinking, *We start now, maybe.*

There was a long minute of uncertainty, during which neither Andy nor Chris moved. Chris' sorrel, alert and uneasy, snorted twice.

Then from out of the circle of firelight, a man's voice said roughly, "Andy, throw your gun away, and then throw his away."

Andy looked at Chris, who nodded. Andy rose, circled the fire on the side away from the man out in the dark, and pulled the worn Colt's .44 from the waistband of Chris' levis and tossed it away from him.

Only then did he remember his orders. He pulled his own gun and pitched it after Chris', and then looked worriedly toward the man in the dark. His plain and now troubled face held small beads of sweat on his upper lip. The content was gone, Chris noted.

There was a movement up the trail, and the tall figure of a man stepped into the firelight and paused. He was a young puncher, tall, wearing worn waist overalls and a blue denim jumper, and his rifle was held at ready across his belly. There was the truculence of the occasion in his dark eyes now, and Chris, not moving, knew he had seen him before when the buggy was halted by Ernie.

Andy said resentfully now, "What's got into you, Bill? That ain't no way to act."

"Shut up, Andy," Bill said contemptuously. His glance was on Chris now, and they studied each other a quiet moment. Bill said then, "We didn't figure you'd have the nerve to try it."

Chris said nothing; he tossed his cigarette in the fire.

"Can't you talk?" Bill demanded.

Chris nodded. "Put down your gun and eat," he said mildly. "I can cut a couple of plugs for the coffeepot."

A look of wild anger crossed Bill's face, as if he had just heard his manhood questioned. "Stand up!" he ordered.

Chris stood up, facing him, attentive and curious now.

"What the hell are you two doin' this close to Thessaly Canyon?"

Chris looked obliquely at Andy. "We close to Thessaly Canyon?"

Andy flushed deeply and nodded. "I short cut it, I reckon. I never figured they'd meet us like this."

Chris looked again at Bill; a disgust stirred within him. Andy, his own man, was so thick he couldn't see the necessity for care or caution even yet! He said quietly, with self-derision, "I was coming up to meet my neighbors."

"You'll meet 'em," Bill said thinly. "Andy, lead your horse over here to me."

Andy silently stepped to the edge of the firelight, but Chris noticed that Bill's rifle was not pointed at Andy, it was pointed at him. They knew Andy pretty well, Chris reflected. Andy was the thick-headed, steady fool, the man without fire or temper, who could always be counted out of any fight, the man nobody had to fear.

They left the clearing headed up the trail, Andy afoot and leading, Chris on Andy's horse, and Bill Arnold on Chris' horse. In this narrow, timbered trail, Chris knew he could not make a break for it unless he rode down Andy, and then his chances of breaking free were slim. He resigned himself. In a few minutes, the trail merged with a newly cut wagon road. Here Bill picked up his own horse and, in the breaking dawn, motioned them up the road.

It was full daylight when they smelled the smoke, then entered the clearing. The creek had swung almost to the side of the canyon, and the cut logs for the cabin lay scattered by the creek like matchsticks. Among them was the chuck wagon, and seated on the logs around it were four members of the Rainbow crew. They were smoking their first cigarettes around the

99

dying fire and finishing their coffee.

As Andy rode into the clearing three of the crew came slowly erect, as men do who are puzzled but not alarmed. The fourth man—Ernie Coombs, Chris saw—came up off his log when Chris rode in, and then, when Bill appeared, he dropped his cup and started slowly around the log toward them. The shack, off to the right, Chris saw, had the four walls head high.

Bill called irritably, "How many times does a man have to fire a shot to get help?"

Nobody answered, understanding it was Bill's quiet brag.

"Get down," Bill said, and Chris dismounted.

Behind Ernie, who was coming toward him, Chris got a glimpse of the broad brown parks among the timber of Thessaly Canyon, and then his attention centered on Ernie as he tried to read the expression in his long face.

Ernie Coombs was grinning faintly as he looked up at Bill. "Where'd you pick 'em up?"

"They built a fire on the trail about a quarter mile below the forks," Bill said, a quiet scorn in his voice.

Ernie looked first at Andy, and Andy looked at the ground like a child reprimanded by a mere look. Then Ernie's attention shifted to Chris, and he was still smiling. "Come to have a look?"

Chris nodded, saying nothing, not liking the way this was shaping up.

"Take a good long look," Ernie said quietly. "You won't want to see it again."

Something in his tone warned the crew. They had been clustered around Ernie; now they scattered, a couple of them drifting behind Chris. Bill reached down for the reins of Chris' sorrel and led him away. Andy, puzzled still, looked from one to the other of the crew.

Ernie said, "You damn tough drifters, you never learn, do you? You been everywhere, you can lick anybody, and you're pretty handy with a six-gun. You can even back down a sheriff once in a while if you find the right sheriff, can't you?" He pulled his gun from its holster and tossed it aside.

Chris saw the anger in Ernie's pale eyes and thought bleakly, *I'm due for a beating.*

He waited until Ernie stepped before him, feet planted wide, and he let Ernie say, "You think you—" before he hit him. Ernie went down and Chris landed on top of him, arms sledging, but it didn't last. Two of the Rainbow hands were on him instantly. They held his arms and wrestled him off Ernie, who scrambled to his feet now, his eyes blazing.

Ernie said, in a shaking voice, "That does it! That'll—"

Ernie ceased talking, his big fists clenched at his sides. He turned his upper body as he looked at Andy West.

"Get on your horse and go home, Nellie," Ernie said sharply.

Andy glanced at Chris, and there was unbelief in his eyes. Chris thought bleakly, *No witnesses,* but he did not speak to Andy. He had tried Andy and found him useless, and his pride held him silent.

"Look here," Andy said. "We didn't do nothing. We—"

"Get your horse!" Ernie said savagely.

Andy gave Chris one despairing look and walked quickly to his horse. He mounted him and turned him and rode into the timber without looking back. Bill drifted his horse over to look down the road, and then turned and nodded to Ernie, who was watching him.

"Get a good hold," Ernie said then to the two men holding Chris.

Chris struggled and Ernie, patient, waited for the two men to wrestle him into submission. Chris stopped presently, breathing hard, his face flushed with the exertion and his gray eyes murderous. Ernie swung then with all the great power of his thick sloping shoulders. Chris saw it coming and turned his head, but Ernie's great sledging blow caught him flush on the jaw hinge. His knees buckled and he sagged in the arms of the two men holding him, dragging them forward to keep their balance.

"Hold him up, hold him up!" Ernie said angrily.

"Hell, he's out," Stew Shallis panted. He stumbled a little on his fat, short legs, and then tripped and fell, and Chris fell slackly with him.

Ernie's eyes were wild now. He stepped forward and grabbed Chris' shirt and lifted, but the shirt tore away in his fingers.

"Damn him!" Ernie said in a whispered, raging voice. "Tough, cocky gun hand!"

His very inability to hurt Chris more held him frustrated and motionless a moment, and then he said savagely, "Get out of the way!" to the man standing beside Chris. He brushed Stew aside roughly and, grasping Chris under the arms, he dragged him over to a nearby log.

Then he looked up at the watching, silent crew. "Come here, Tip. Come here!"

A plain-faced puncher stepped over to him, and Ernie reached down and lifted Chris' arm so that his right hand lay atop the log. "Hold it that way," Ernie said.

Tip, bewildered, knelt and held Chris' hand as he was instructed, and when the hand lay flat on the log, Ernie raised his foot and stamped savagely on Chris' hand.

Tip dropped Chris' arm as if it were hot and looked up, and Ernie said wrathfully, "Put it back! Put it back!"

Tip did, and Ernie stamped three more times, the sharp high heel of his boot thudding with a thick muffled sound on Chris' hand and skidding off each time, ripping a great furrow in the skin.

He paused then, his eyes still bright with fury, and looked down at Chris. Then, slowly, he lifted his gaze to the silent sober crew.

Tip stood up, watching Chris' arm slide off the log and flop across his belly. It was bleeding freely now.

Ernie said, "That's the way to treat these tough drifters, break their gun hand. Watch him dog it out of the country now."

He made it sound as if only bare justice had been done, and it took the crew scarcely a moment to adjust their beliefs to his. They came up and looked at Chris, and Ernie quietly rolled a smoke, not taking his eyes from Chris' face.

"You must have broke his hand," one man observed. "He never moved."

"He'll move," Ernie said grimly. "Throw him in the shack where we can watch him, and then get to work."

A scalding, formless abasement that he didn't know was anger built up in Andy as he rode down the wagon road. Something was happening back there, something they didn't want him to see, and it was happening to Danning. The very violence of what he tried to imagine sickened Andy for a moment. He didn't try to define his feeling toward Danning, but behind his anger and loyalty now was a deep sense of guilt. Danning had trusted him, and he had blundered them both into a stupid trap. And Danning was taking his medicine. What were they doing to him that they didn't want him to see? Shooting him? Maiming him? In the past few minutes, the world Andy had always shut his eyes to lay naked and fearful before him. He longed for the gun that he carried only because everyone else did, with a passion that made him reach for his empty holster.

And then the thought came to him. Bill Arnold hadn't picked up their guns; they were still at the camp. Andy spurred his horse and went straight to his gun lying in the brown-black humus of pine needles. Turning, he ran back toward his horse, and then hauled up and looked about him. If one gun was good, two were better. He found the second six-gun and rammed it in the waistband of his pants. Mounting now, he turned his horse and again put him at a run up the trail.

At the forks now, he had cunning enough to rein up and plan his course, haste or no haste. He rode on a ways, and when he could hear the clean chunk of ax blows in the air, he pulled off the road and tied his horse to a tree and went on afoot, circling through the timber until he reached the creek.

They were working. What had happened to Chris? Walking as silently as he could, half running when he thought the sound of the chopping would cover the noise he made, he came to the edge of the clearing, and halted some feet back in the timber. He could see the crew now.

Bill Arnold and chunky Stew Shallis had just laid down a log and were still bent over, listening to Tip Henry who stood in the doorway of the half-raised cabin. Ernie and Rossiter were seated on a log, their backs to him. Now they rose and went over to Tip, and Bill and Stew tramped over, too. Was Danning in there?

Andy noted carefully that only Ernie wore his gun.

He walked softly toward the camp and, leaving the trees, stepped over the first log as he heard Ernie say loudly, "Like your neighbors, hardcase?"

Andy halted, raised both guns hip high, and said in an angry, choked voice, "The whole lot of you turn around!"

They all turned to look at him now, unmoving in their surprise; Bill Arnold, after a moment's puzzlement, accounted for the guns and said softly, "Well, I'm damned!"

Ernie Coombs said mildly, "Be careful of those things, Andy. They go off." And he started for Andy, a smile on his long face but a look of caution in his eyes.

Andy tilted one gun a bare half inch and let the hammer off. The slug slapped into the top log of the shack. Ernie stopped cold in his tracks, the smile fading from his face.

"You damn fool!" Ernie said. "We can get a U. S. Marshal on you for that. This is a Government homestead!"

"Bill," Andy said, "throw Ernie's gun away."

Bill Arnold was scared, Andy saw, and it gave him a sense of confidence and power as Bill came up beside Coombs and threw Ernie's gun in the grass.

Ernie said thinly, "Go on, go on, get yourself in some real trouble."

Andy didn't answer him. He circled Ernie and Bill, waved Shallis and Tip and Ed over beside them, and then briefly looked in at the chip-laden, grassy floor of the shack. Chris was on his hands and knees, trying to push himself to his feet. Andy saw his bloody hand, and a hot anger boiled up in him.

"You! Tip and Stew! Help him down to the creek!"

The two came forward and got Chris. As they passed him on the way to the creek, Andy noted Chris' head hung deep on his chest and his lagging directionless step, and he said with the slow-forming decision of a man who seldom has to make one, "I think I'm going to shoot you, Ernie."

Ernie laughed, and Bill Arnold stepped carefully away from him. He had seen the mule look in Andy's face, and did not like it. Ernie said now in a bold and confident voice, "Go ahead, make yourself trouble, Andy. Get hung on account of a tough drifter."

Andy's glance shuttled to the creek. Chris was on his knees in the water, clumsily scooping water with his good hand onto his face and his hair and onto the back of his neck. His other hand lay in the water.

Ernie's speech was a little hurried now—smooth and persuasive and softly Texan and reasonable. "Andy, you don't know what you're doin'. This is land protected by the law. You and that saddle tramp are as good as in the pen now if we want to report you. Now take him and get out of here, and I'll tell Miles to forget it."

Andy still watched Chris. He saw him come to his feet, shake the water from his hair and then turn to face them, and his wet and shining face held a look that made Andy afraid again. Chris walked out of the creek, his wet clothes clinging to him. Then his pace increased, and he was heading straight for Ernie. There was a kind of indomitable fury in him as he stumbled once and caught himself and then broke into a run.

When Ernie swung at him as he came on, Chris did not even pause. He butted Ernie in the face with his head and kneed him savagely in the groin, and Ernie went over backwards, tripping over a log. Chris, too, tripped on the log and sprawled, face down, but even as he fell his feet were driving him forward, always forward. Ernie yelled and rolled over, and Chris came at him with the ferocity of a demented animal. Ernie struck at him and kicked at him, wild in panic, but could not stop him.

When Chris hit him with his body and wrapped both arms about him and lifted him up, Ernie smashed down at his head with fisted hands as if he were driving nails with a hammer.

Chris threw him forward and followed him down, and they fell on a log which caught Ernie in the small of the back. His breath was driven from him in a great shuddering cough.

Chris had never let go of him; now he pulled himself astride Ernie and put his right forearm under his chin and bent Ernie's head back and down, so that Ernie's back was bowed over the log. Again and again, Chris drove sledging, wild blows at his face and Ernie struggled convulsively, kicking wildly. Suddenly his struggling stopped.

Then Chris took the pressure off his chin and slugged

again, and this time, because Ernie's face was where he could hit it and he was still blind with his fury, Chris forgot and drove his right hand into Ernie's face.

The shock and pain of it brought a low groan from him and, still astride Ernie, Chris hugged the hand to his chest and bent his head, waiting for the pain to go. It was then Bill Arnold broke for the brush, and Andy let him go.

All of them now, Andy included, walked slowly toward Chris. His hand still hugged to his breast, Chris turned and came off Ernie, who slid to a sitting position on the ground and fell over on his side.

Chris' face was bloodless with the pain, but his eyes, Andy noticed, were still crazy mad.

Chris held his hurt hand out and looked at the Rainbow men, and he swayed unsteadily on his feet as he asked, "How'd he do it?"

Stew Shallis tried to speak and no words came out. He cleared his throat and said in a thin phlegmy voice, "Stomped on it."

Chris turned back to Ernie then and pulled him over so he was on his face, arms outflung. He put his foot on Ernie's right wrist, and with his left boot he stamped solidly time and again on the back of Ernie's hand. Ernie jerked convulsively, soundlessly, and subsided.

Chris lifted his wild gaze again now to the Rainbow crew, and was silent a moment as he carefully cradled his crippled hand against his chest.

Presently he said, "Which one of you is Tip Henry?"

There was a long pause and Tip Henry said, "That's me."

Chris slowly extended his injured hand now and pointed at Tip, his arm straight and unwavering and sighted like a gun. "You homesteaded this place for Miles, Tip," Chris said. "You'll live on it a year, and half those nights I'll come back here and shoot it up until you move or I kill you. Get off it!"

His hand fell to his side, and was drawn up against his chest immediately. Cradling it thus, his eyes now sought Andy. "Andy, find me my horse."

Chapter VIII

When Miles left the hotel dining room after dinner that noon, Big Ben Lavendar beckoned him from one of the lobby chairs where he was talking, and Younger went over. He shook hands with Ben, who had a ranch out north by the dune country, and said hello to Travis, a small scholarly looking man who did surveying work at the mines up around Petrie in the Blackbows. Waycross, who owned the hardware store and was postmaster, winked solemnly at him. They were competitors, but Younger had made it a point to keep his friendship.

Ben Lavendar said, "Sorry to hear about Sam. Truscott showed me the letter." His broad, wind-ruddied face showed a concern that Younger tried to match in his own expression. Ben Lavendar, with

Truscott and Walt Hardison, made up the board of commissioners.

"A rest will do him good," Younger said soberly.

"I'm glad you can spare that young redhead," Ben went on. "Good man. Wish he'd marry my daughter, if I had a daughter."

Younger laughed with the rest of them and went on out. Crossing over to the store, he smiled faintly. Mac was in, as O'Hea's deputy. The talk this noon in the dining room had confirmed Lavendar's opinion. Only Walt Hardison was against it, and he, Younger reflected, couldn't do anything about it. He tramped back through the main aisle of the store, pausing only to speak to a couple of punchers from Crowfoot, his neighbor to the west.

Back in the office, he shucked out of his coat and stretched lazily. The flat ropes of muscle across his shoulders stretched his white shirt almost to the tearing point. He saw the stack of ledgers MacElvey had set on his desk for the monthly review of the status of his affairs, which were prospering.

Closing the door he sat down, half turned his chair to the window and began going over the books. This, after all, was the deepest pleasure he knew. In them he could read a story that was completely personal and delightful, the story of his own wisdom and shrewdness. For instance, he saw now where the sum he had spent setting up the tie-cutting camp over on the south slope of the Blackbows was going to be sufficient, according to Mac's report. The crew was ahead of schedule, and his contract with the railroad for several thousand ties would be met well within the deadline and he could clear close to eighteen hundred dollars. He thought of that with pleasure and tried to remember the exact sum of the original investment.

Minutes later, he mentally hauled himself up; he hadn't been thinking of Mac's figures, he'd been thinking of Danning. Shaking his head, as if to reprove himself, he turned now to Mac's estimate on the Sulinam job. It was in a separate folder, its pages well thumbed, its contents known to him by heart. For this was his boldest gamble, and it involved his whole future. A stamp mill was being built in Case Valley out on the flats thirty miles to the west of Triumph to service the dozen mines scattered nearby in the Blackbows. The Sulinam mine above Petrie was in an almost inaccessible spot high in the Blackbows, perched on a big deposit of only medium-grade gold ore, and with the building of the Case Valley stamp mill, Sulinam had seen the possibility of working their medium-grade deposits. Accordingly, Sulinam had asked for bids on the moving of 175,000 tons of ore from its mine to the Case Valley stamp mill. Whoever got the contract would have to build a road and haul out over it, in big ore wagons. The outlay of money for the wagons, for the teams, for the blacksmith shops, for the buildings, for the crews, for the feed, for the commissary, the road crews, the tools, the surveying and maintenance, had at first disheartened Younger. It was too big for him to handle, he had believed, and the time limit to completion too short. But Mac, who seemed to know something of everything, had broken down the cost figures, and had shown Younger how it could be done. By sending his own man south into good horse country and by paying cash for horses, he could get his teams cheaply. By paying cash for second-hand wagons, he could get the wagons at a bargain figure. By using his tie-camp crew for cutting the road, he could pare the cost of the road down to a fraction of what other contractors would have to spend, and be well within the time limit.

And Younger, in the end, had decided to gamble. He had mortgaged Rainbow to get the cash, and borrowed steeply, but if he got the contract Mac had shown him that he would be a rich man. The bid would be let next Monday morning, now, and Younger, with Mac's figures memorized, knew for certain that his bid would be low. If it was not, nothing was lost. Already, Dan Fairshine had the horses chosen, and Sholtz had found the wagons; they only awaited telegrams that Miles' bid was low to put down the cash and quickly start in motion the whole machinery which, when it was finally working smoothly, would mean Younger was on his way to becoming a rich man.

Younger studied the folder now, but again his mind wandered to Danning, and this time he let it. He pondered Danning's probable first move. Whatever it was, it would be bound to get him in trouble, for Younger had been unable to find a chink in his own armor. But if that were so, why did he feel so uneasy? He remembered Mac's question, "Have you known him?" and again he wondered. *I've covered up,* he thought grimly. *Not a one of them got out of it, not even the woman on the stage. Tana didn't know me, and he's dead; the old man's dead and even the Army's given up.*

He heard the door open and he looked up irritably, the residue of the worry still on his face. It was a stern face, cruel now with temper and irritability, and his dark secret thoughts had made his eyes ugly. This was what Abbie saw when she stepped in, and it stopped her abruptly in the doorway. The expression on Younger's face was only fleeting, and it vanished immediately. An expression of indifference replaced it—that and a quick appraising glance at her clothes.

"I'm busy," Younger said.

"All right. You're never alone, though, and I wanted to tell you something." She smiled faintly and added, "About business, so don't yawn."

Younger was yawning. He finished it, unmoved by her jibe, and shoved the folder onto the desk and leaned back in his chair.

Abbie wore a light frilly dress with red ribbon threaded through the hem of the skirt. Her parasol which matched it, she laid across MacElvey's desk and sat down in his chair.

Younger watching her, said, "Seen your father?"

Abbie nodded. "He told me you told him to write the letter."

114

"I did. It's either sick leave for him or take his medicine. Mrs. Harms has already spread the story of what happened at Henhouse. The next puncher that gets liquored up at Melaven's will hooraw your father out of town. A sheriff has got to make his orders stick or get out."

"I suppose that's true," Abbie said quietly, her dark eyes watchful and alert. "That doesn't mean his salary stops, does it?"

"No. He'll draw salary. I'll pay Mac's." Younger smiled unpleasantly. "I'll keep him pensioned, if that's what's worrying you."

Anger flickered in Abbie's dark eyes. "You'll keep him pensioned or your wife will go back to baking pies, Younger."

"All right, all right; he's taken care of," Younger said irritably. "He's still sheriff, too. Now what do you want?"

"Has Frank Yordy seen you?"

"Yordy? No. Why would he?"

"He said he wanted to, told me to tell you. He thinks you'll want to buy some information about the Harms place he claims to have." She paused. "I hope you kick him off the walk."

Younger grunted. "I know more about the Henhouse than he'll ever know." He frowned. "When'd he see you?"

"After Danning threw him off the place yesterday. He said he'd be at Briggs' place for three or four days. He wanted you to ride out." Abbie rose now and

115

picked up her parasol. "He's a four-flusher, Younger, and he'll get you in trouble."

"With my own sheriff?" Younger asked dryly.

"All right, but—"

"Sure, sure," Younger cut in brusquely. "I don't even want to see him. Now let me alone, will you?"

He reached for the folder again and Abbie went out of the office without bidding him good-by, closing the door behind her.

Younger opened the folder, then looked at the wall, speculating idly on what Yordy wanted of him. He'd told Abbie the truth; he knew everything about Henhouse there was to know. He knew Della had borrowed money from Truscott with which to feed that bunch of two-year-olds she was holding through the winter. Now there was an idea so half-witted it would take Yordy and a couple of women to think it up, he reflected. He also knew that Della and her mother made a poor living once the crew was paid off, and he knew further that they would make a lot poorer living once they'd lost Thessaly and a couple of other spots whose grass he could move in on legally. No, there was nothing Yordy could tell him.

He went back to his books, Yordy forgotten, and was interrupted again only when the clerk stuck his head in at six o'clock to say good night.

Younger finished quickly, yawned, stretched, put on his coat and hat and went out into the street. He turned up it and went into Melaven's corner saloon for his nightly drink. The bar was against the south wall, and a scattering of customers were bellied up to it. The tile floor was cool and white, yet its whiteness did not disturb the pleasant gloom of the place, which was now lighted against the dusk of the street. A couple of men were playing cribbage at one of the six big card tables which lined the windows opposite the bar, and the rest of the tables were empty.

Miles walked over to the bar and said, "Hello, Hughie," to the short, florid-faced Irishman tending bar. Out of habit, he read again the framed sign on the back bar, "If you can't stand up on a tile floor, you're drunk. Go home," and accepted the bottle of whisky Melaven set before him, and poured a drink.

Melaven said, "I hear O'Hea's finally took leave, poor fella."

Younger nodded and took his drink, and Melaven, seeing Younger was not in a conversational mood, moved off to other customers.

Younger was pouring his second drink when he heard the sharp footfalls on the tile floor of a man walking in a hurry. He looked over his shoulder and saw Tip Henry approaching, and he signaled to Melaven for another glass.

Tip said, "Howdy, Younger," and Younger smiled, saying, "It'll keep, Tip. Take a drink first."

Tip Henry grinned worriedly, poured his drink and downed it with a reflective smack of his lips. He looked around him then and Younger picked up the bottle and said, "Bring your glass," and sauntered over to the end card table where they could have privacy.

They sat down in the barrel chairs and Younger tipped his hat back on his forehead and relaxed comfortably. "What's the hurry, Tip?"

Tip told him about Danning's visit that morning. He told it all, sparing none of the details, and as he talked he watched the hard glint of anger move into Younger's eyes. Finished, he waited, and Younger slowly turned his whisky glass on the table top, his eyes speculative, secret, angry. "Where's Ernie?" he asked, without looking up.

"We got him down to the house. He's there now. I'm supposed to get Doc Evans out there."

"Then go get him," Younger said, still looking at his whisky glass.

Tip didn't move. He took a deep breath, watching Younger, and when Younger looked up at him, Tip said, "Another thing, Younger. You won't like this either."

"What?"

"I'm quittin'."

A raw rage was in Younger's face then. It came swiftly and Tip knew a real alarm as he watched it come and then go. "Scared of him?" Younger asked.

"You are damn right," Tip said flatly. "That's the word for it. I'm scared."

Younger didn't say anything, only looked at him, and Tip said, again flatly, "He's an Injun. He's crazy!"

Younger moved the bottle of whisky out of his way and leaned his arm on the table. "I took you over to Moorehouse and helped you file on that place, Tip. I paid your fee, I'm payin' you good wages, I'm feedin' you and I'm payin' you a thousand dollars for a quarter section when you've proved up on it. All right, if that's not enough, I'll meet your figure. Any figure."

"You don't get it," Tip said patiently. "There ain't enough money in the world to keep me there. I'm quittin', I tell you. I ain't ever goin' back there. He'll kill me."

"I'll put four men with you every night."

"He'll kill them, too. I tell you, he's crazy."

Miles said bitterly, "You haven't got title to it until you've proved up on it, so you can't transfer it. Where does that leave me?"

"I dunno. It leaves me alive, though."

"No!" Younger shook his head in violent contradiction. "The first time he shoots at you, he'll be hunted down by a U. S. Marshal. Hell, we can hunt him down ourselves!"

"What good does that do with me dead?" Tip demanded. "He wasn't talking to you, Younger; he wasn't talkin' to Ernie or none of them. He was talking to me." Tip tapped his chest with his index finger again and again, his eyes dead serious.

Younger leaned back in his chair and said softly, "Well, I'm damned."

But Tip was through arguing. He said respectfully, "Can I get my time now?"

Younger looked at him a long moment and then said, "See MacElvey."

Tip stood up and awkwardly thrust out his hand.

119

"It's been a good job, Younger."

Younger said in a low, wicked voice, "Get out of here, Tip, before I hurt you."

Tip flushed and turned away and walked out of the saloon. Younger sat motionless, staring morosely at the bottle, his eyes still hot. The blame for it lay on Ernie Coombs, of course, and he was glad Ernie had got what was coming to him. But the result affected him, and he could write Thessaly Canyon off now. At the end of a year, when Tip failed to prove up on his homestead, it would be open to filing again, but a year was a long time to wait, too long. Henhouse had won the first move, thanks to Danning. Younger wondered with a savage scorn how any man could be so terrified of another that he would do what Tip had done. He rose now, remembering Tip's errand, and he hoped Doc Evans wouldn't have any mercy on Ernie.

Paying his score he went out, heading for the hotel where Doc Evans customarily took his supper. He was in the hotel and halfway across the lighted lobby when he saw Dr. Evans, small and spry and cheerful, come out of the dining room.

He stopped him and said, "Doc, we got a man hurt out at Rainbow. Can you run on out?"

Dr. Evans said matter-of-factly, "What's the matter with your man, Younger?"

Younger made a vague circling gesture with his hand. "Broken hand, busted nose. I don't rightly know."

"Broken hand," Dr. Evans said. He paused and said,

"Two broken hands the same day. How'd that happen?"

"I can tell you how it didn't happen," Younger said grimly. "They weren't shaking hands."

Doc raised his eyebrows, shrugged and went out, and Younger drifted out after him and strolled to the edge of the boardwalk. The street lay in the full brightness of the low sun, so that he could even see the nails in the false front of Canning's saddle shop across the street. There was no traffic now and the street was so quiet that he could hear the sound of someone sawing wood on the edge of town. A morose restlessness was on him; he wanted to get off by himself and think this out. The legal way, the respectable way was not going to work, he knew now, and the next move must be a careful one.

He walked down to the corner and stood there aimlessly for a moment, wanting to get moving and wondering whether he should wait for Dr. Evans. He decided against waiting and went down to the livery and got his horse, leaving word there for Dr. Evans that he had gone on ahead.

Younger rode a big vicious black that, now Younger mounted him, danced sideways down the livery center way and bolted out into the quiet street. Younger let him run to the edge of town and hauled him up roughly. He was not in a mood to enjoy the sharp edge of his horse's temper at the moment, and he kept him at a walk past the last straggling houses of the town.

At the edge of town he met a dirty, unshaven

puncher astride a good bay horse and, as they drew even, the puncher said respectfully, "Howdy, Younger."

"Hello, Briggs," Younger answered indifferently, and made no move to stop and pass the time of day. The sun was far down now and the flats clear to the Blackbows were touched with a pale bright light. Younger glanced over at his shadow which extended far off the road, dark and elongated, and he felt an odd depression. It galled him to think that he had the money, the law behind him, and the plan, and it all counted for nothing in the face of one man's stubbornness. He'd found his country and his people, and he was going to be one of them—big and powerful, feared a little, but above all, respected, so that when he died they'd feel a hole in their lives. Danning wasn't going to stop him, but how to get rid of Danning without risking the whole business was another matter.

Certainly, he reflected, there was a way, a legal way, to shove a tottering, two-bit outfit like Henhouse over the brink into ruin. Either the men who worked for them could be bought, or—and then he remembered Yordy.

As he thought of Yordy, he remembered Abbie saying he would be at Briggs'. When he thought of it, he half turned in his saddle, as if to speak to Briggs who was gone these ten minutes past. Then he looked ahead of him and saw Briggs' small shack off across the flats. He hadn't passed Briggs' road yet, and as he rode on he wondered if Yordy would be there now. He didn't like the man, didn't trust him, but what if Yordy, for once in his life, talked sense?

When he came to the wagon road into Briggs' place, he reined up, hesitant, and then, almost reluctantly, he turned in. Briggs' place was a sty, and approaching it, Younger's nose quivered in distaste. It was a one-room shack surrounded by a tangle of corrals whose poles were so high they almost hid the sagging shack roof. Joe Briggs was a horse trader and horse breaker and sometimes horse hunter. If he was also a horse stealer, nobody had proven it yet. But his corrals were always full of horses of all ages and colors, and bearing strange brands, and they were all cleaner than he was. Among the more shiftless lot of punchers and small ranchers Briggs enjoyed a reputation as a wit, an astute judge of horses and a drinking companion.

As Younger rode up into the bare dusty yard between the corrals, he thought the place was deserted. He pulled his horse around; the big black kicked a can, of which there were dozens scattered about the yard, and a moment later Yordy came to the door.

He saw Younger riding out and called, "Younger, you lookin' for anybody?"

Younger pulled his horse around and came back. Reining up in front of the door, he made no effort to dismount but only stared curiously at Yordy.

Yordy, obviously, had been on a drunk, and was still

drinking. His eyes were red-rimmed and pouchy, and his loose soft face held the high flush of alcohol.

"Mrs. Miles said you were looking for me," Younger said coldly.

Yordy grinned knowingly. "I figured you'd come. Light and step in and have a drink."

Younger said rudely, "What do you want to see me about? I'm in a hurry."

"Didn't she tell you?"

"No."

Again Yordy grinned. "All right, I'll be a sucker. All the same, she did."

Younger was tempted to ride off without another word, and it must have showed in his face, for Yordy put a hand on the door jamb and leaned on it and said in a low voice, "What's it worth to you to have Henhouse so flat broke them women'll quit?"

"Not much."

Yordy snorted. "Like hell."

They regarded each other in silence, and Younger shook a foot free from the stirrup and leaned his folded arms on the saddle horn, first shoving his hat to the back of his head in the timeless gesture of the bargainer on horseback.

"You're bluffing, Yordy. I know everything about Henhouse you do. There's nothing you can tell me."

"I can tell you how to break 'em," Yordy reiterated. "It's safe, too."

"How?"

Yordy snorted. "Let's talk money first."

"What kind of money?"

"Say, five hundred dollars," Yordy said bluntly.

Younger could tell that Yordy would be satisfied with a third of that, but he said calmly, "It's a deal. Five hundred—*if* I like the idea, and *if* it's safe. But who's judge of that?"

Yordy was so surprised and so pleased his sum had been accepted that he said promptly, "You are. I'll trust you. Besides, I'll know whether or not you used it."

"Then let's have it."

Yordy stepped out of the doorway and looked around him in the unconscious gesture of a man about to impart a secret. Then he squinted up at Younger and said, "You know that box canyon below the falls there on Elder Creek?"

Younger, frowning, nodded.

"Well, Della's kept that fenced off all summer to keep the feed. The grass there's shoulder high to a man in some places, and all of it's sun-cured. Well, we turned that bunch of two-year-olds in there the other day, the whole lot of 'em. You know about 'em?"

Again Younger nodded, his eyes attentive.

"She's borrowed on them cattle for feed. A lot of money, too. You know that?"

"Everyone does."

Yordy's grin came back. "Suppose some night one of your boys was to touch a match to that brush fence. It'd set off the grass, and that grass will burn like pitch. Them cattle will move ahead of it right up to the

125

dead end of the box canyon and when the fire gets up there—" He spread his hands, watching Younger.

Miles didn't answer for a full minute, turning this over in his mind. It was, he saw immediately, a pretty thing. He'd seen grass fires in Texas, and they were death to anything in their way. If Della lost that bunch, moreover, she couldn't begin to meet Truscott's note. Either she'd have to sell a chunk of Henhouse, or it would go to Truscott. In either event, it would be his eventually. As for the risk involved, it was negligible. And even though this was a dry summer in the mountains, the fire would be confined to Falls Canyon. Even if it jumped the rim, it was so close to timber line the fire could burn itself out and not do much damage. Altogether, it was pretty.

He said quietly, "Who've you told this to, Briggs?"

"And let him sell it to you? Hell, I'm more'n five years old," Yordy said indignantly.

Younger believed him, but, after the fire what would Yordy have to gain by keeping silent, once his money was gone? More money, of course. He would be a source of constant blackmail, and sooner or later on one of his drunks he would tattle. Yordy would have to be got out of the country, or out of the way. And when Younger had that thought a faint pounding excitement crept into his blood. He sat there, eyes inward looking, rapt in thought for so long that Yordy shifted his feet and cleared his throat.

Presently, Younger looked at him again. "I'll buy it," he said softly. "You leave the country, of course."

"I've got a fiddle-foot, and all I need is the money," Yordy agreed.

Younger came erect. "You'll leave the country two nights from now," he said. "I'll meet you at Station with the money and I'll see you over the pass."

"Fair enough," Yordy agreed, smiling. "Let's have a drink on it."

"I don't need a drink on it," Younger said flatly. "Neither do you. I'll tell you why you don't, Yordy. Because I'd hate to have you get drunk and tell this to Briggs, so Briggs could collect after you've gone. I'd hate to have Joe Briggs hanged for a horse thief and you hanged for his partner. Remember who's sheriff here? And deputy sheriff?"

"You can't talk to me like that," Yordy said sullenly.

"Why can't I?"

When Yordy didn't answer, Younger said, "Sunday night at Station. Have your stuff ready and be on the hotel porch." He nodded and put the spurs to his black horse, and this time he let him run.

Chapter IX

Kate usually ate ahead of the crowd at noon so that later she could keep an eye on the two waitresses and act as cashier. She had taken a chair at the table closest the kitchen and was chatting with one of the girls who was finishing setting the tables, when Perry MacElvey came into the dining room.

127

He walked over to the table where Kate was seated and, because she liked him, she said teasingly, "How is it going, Sheriff?"

"The public hasn't stoned me yet," Mac said, with quiet self-derision, and gave her one of his rare smiles.

Kate wondered then, as she had wondered in the past, what MacElvey had been and seen and done in his life. He never talked of himself, and all the town knew about him was that he was a city man come west for his health. But there was a history of breeding and ability in him; he was a man, like her father, whom people trusted immediately and turned to for help. And help was given, Kate knew, and that was what puzzled her. How could a man like Mac, generous and kind, work for Younger Miles, whose every move was calculated to serve his own interests? Thinking of that, she remembered what she had been pondering ever since she'd heard of O'Hea's sick leave and Mac's appointment, and she resolved to go ahead with it.

But before she could speak, the first of the diners came through the door. She knew they would, out of courtesy, fill up her table first and she said to Mac, "Where'll you be this afternoon, sheriff? I want some advice."

Mac looked skeptically at her. "In O'Hea's office. But why would you come to me for advice when your father's a couple of dozen steps away?"

"This is different," Kate said.

Younger Miles and John Truscott, the thin, worried-looking man who ran the First National Bank, came in first. Miles saw Mac and led the way over to Kate's table, and Kate spoke pleasantly to them both. Younger sat next to her, Truscott next him, and they were served. There was some small talk of the weather and Truscott groused about the dry year, claiming there wasn't enough grass in the world to feed the cattle he'd made loans on this year.

"There'll be a lot of hands turned loose this fall," Younger said. "No grass, no beef. No beef, no money. No money, no crew."

Truscott nodded. "I paid Frank Yordy off the other day for Box H. He said some unkind things about the country in general, too."

"Drunken fool," Younger murmured. "He's a man with a grudge; he stopped my wife a couple of days ago and said he had some information he wanted to sell me. Some information, mind you, that would hurt Box H."

He looked around the table, and Truscott said:

"That's like him."

Kate, always practical, said, "What did you do?"

"I went out to Briggs' place to tell him to drop that kind of talk or he'd get in trouble. I was curious about what he wanted to sell me, though."

"Yes," Kate said, innocently.

Younger looked sharply at her, but there was only interest in her pale brown eyes.

"I finally got it out of him. He had figured out that Danning was all that propped up Box H. Get rid of Danning and the Harms women would quit."

"And how did he propose to do it?" Kate asked, interested now.

Younger made a wry face. "It seems back of their place there's a trail up onto the bench that cuts through a shale slide." He looked at Truscott, Kate and MacElvey. "Yordy said it would be very easy to start a shale slide some time when Danning was passing. No evidence—and no Danning."

Kate put down her fork. "How horrible," she said, softly.

Younger said bluntly, "I feel that way too, Kate. I told Yordy I'd pass on his suggestion to the sheriff." He looked at MacElvey. "I'm hereby passing it, Mac. You might warn Danning, too."

MacElvey nodded, and the conversation changed to other things.

Kate finished, excused herself and went out. She busied herself at the desk, making change, but Yordy's plan to finish Danning kept returning, sickening her with its wanton cruelty. When the last diner had eaten and left, Kate went out into the street to keep her date with MacElvey. She was bareheaded, and sun, touching her hair, gave it little fiery lights of gold.

Abe Wildman, teetering on his heels in front of Melaven's, grinned and said as she came up, "It's a good thing you don't have pigtails, Kate, or they'd have you back in school."

"You know how to compliment a lady, Abe," Kate said in her friendly way. "How are you?"

"Fine, lookin' at you. Fine."

Kate smiled and passed him and walked up the street. She waved to Mrs. Waycross and another woman on the opposite boardwalk who were carrying parasols, and then laughed to herself. She treated the town as her own back yard, she thought, and she tried to remember when she had last thought it necessary to wear a hat or carry a parasol. Passing the high lumberyard fence, she turned into the sheriff's office and passed the first door and entered the second.

Crossing the anteroom, she could see MacElvey seated in O'Hea's old swivel chair reading. He came to his feet when she entered and pulled a chair over for her, facing his own.

"Why don't you open this corridor door and close up that filthy room, now you're sheriff?" Kate asked him.

"It's open. Did you try it?" Mac asked.

Kate laughed at herself and said no, and sat down. Mac sank into the swivel chair again, waiting courteously for her to begin.

"I suppose you've guessed what I wanted to talk to you about," Kate began. "It's Abbie."

"I hadn't guessed it," Mac said. "I might have. You're a good friend of hers, aren't you?"

"Can't a man be punished for selling her liquor?"

Mac shook his head in negation, his green eyes polite, sympathetic.

"Then can't you find who's doing it and threaten him or—or—something?" Kate asked. "This can't go on, Mac."

"It can if she wants it to," Mac said quietly. He picked a pencil off the desk and stabbed aimlessly with it at a pile of papers on the desk top. He looked up at her presently and said, "I'm no judge of why she drinks, but she needs liquor. She's got the need, she's got the money, and she's got the cunning. And I'm not the sheriff of her morals, Kate."

"You make me out a busybody," Kate said.

"I've got to. It's Younger's and her business, not mine, and, pardon me—not yours."

"I know. But if I only knew who sold her the liquor."

Mac shrugged. "What if you did? It's no crime. She could write to any distillery and they'd send her a barrel. Maybe," he said dryly, "that's what she's done."

They regarded each other levelly, and Kate could see the stubbornness in the man. She knew she was asking him to meddle, perhaps dangerously, but in a good cause; he had told her he sympathized, but that he refused. Or did he even sympathize? She tried to read what lay behind those quiet green eyes, and she could not, and suddenly the absurdity of her request struck her. She kept forgetting Mac was Younger Miles' man. Like him as she might, she knew he would never cross Younger—and this was crossing Younger.

She gathered her feet under her to rise when the sound of footfalls in the corridor came to them. The corridor door opened immediately and Chris Danning stepped into the room. *It's like him, to try that door,*

132

Kate thought instantly. *He won't do anything like other people do.* She noted first the bandaged hand at his side. It was thick in its splint, hiding the whole hand, except the square fingertips, and was already slightly soiled.

He stood in the doorway a moment, and then took off his soft, worn hat that looked as if it had been bleached by all the sun of the desert.

There was a cut on his lean, sun-blackened cheek, but his eyes, Kate saw, were the same—the palest of gray, deep-set, with a go-to-hell look in them that was like the flick of a whip to a person beholding them. She had heard about the fight, and she had hoped that Ernie Coombs had altered that look, making it more respectful. He hadn't.

Chris said, unsmilingly, "I'll come back later."

Kate stood up. "Don't go. I'm just leaving." She turned to Mac. "Thanks for nothing, Mac. I shouldn't have bothered you."

Mac almost smiled. "You shouldn't have bothered yourself."

Kate started for the door, but Danning didn't move out of the way. He said, "I wonder if you'd be my witness, Miss Hardison?"

"Witness? To what?"

Chris' glance shifted to Mac. "You sheriff now?"

"Deputy," Mac said. "O'Hea's on sick leave. I'm acting in his place."

"Is Thessaly Canyon open range?" Chris asked.

Mac nodded. "Except for the quarter section Tip

133

Henry's staked out at the mouth of it."

"I'm moving Box H stuff into it through the upper trail," Chris said. "I figured I'd tell you."

Mac was quiet a long moment, and then said, "Rainbow's using it. The practice, I think, is to stay off open range used by another outfit."

"I'm moving *back* to it," Chris said slowly. "We used it once, we're using it now. Tell Miles what the practice is; I know already."

"My friend," Mac said mildly, "you're headed for trouble. You've given nobody around here cause to love you. This is Miles you're talking about," he continued, a faint stirring of anger in his voice. "You're a marked man. Yordy is already trying to peddle ways to kill you."

"That's likely," Chris agreed calmly. "To Miles, I suppose?"

"Yes, to Miles," Mac said.

Chris' glance returned now to Kate. "Thank you, Miss Hardison. You might tell your father what I just told MacElvey."

He stood aside and Kate waved to Mac and went out. Chris stepped out too, closing the door behind him. It would put him on the boardwalk two paces behind her, and Kate decided to wait for him. She was still astonished at what she had just witnessed and the news she had heard, and when he fell into step beside her, she said, "You know, you have a way about you. It's a little bit like a sledge hammer, but I think it works."

She looked up at him beside her, and for the first time she could remember, he looked as if once, long ago and far, far away, he had known how to smile. A veiled and cautious amusement was in his eyes as he regarded her, but his face was still stern. "It works," he said quietly.

"That took some courage in a brassy way," Kate said, reflectively. "So does moving into Thessaly. Are you going to?"

"We did. This morning."

"But you— Weren't you hurt? Didn't Della bring you in last night?"

Chris only nodded and held up his hand a moment for answer and dropped it.

"What—what happened to you?"

"I broke my hand."

"All right," Kate said in exasperation. "You make me ask questions, so I'll ask them. How did it happen?"

"Ernie Coombs stamped on it," Chris answered.

Kate looked up at him swiftly, but his expression was only polite. "And what did you do to Ernie?"

"I broke his hand," Chris replied.

Kate halted on the boardwalk, and Chris stopped too. Kate was about to speak, and closed her mouth, and then did speak. "By stamping on it, I'll bet. That's like you. I should have known that." There was, oddly, no censure in her voice.

She turned and began to walk again, and Chris, saying nothing, walked beside her. Kate, much against

135

her judgment, felt a strange and compelling liking for the man at the moment. She remembered their last meeting, when each of them had tried to be as unkind to the other as possible. But to know that he had come out of his second tangle with Rainbow with the same conviction that he, alone, could lick Younger Miles was somewhat magnificent, if foolish. And he had gone about proving it by moving in on Thessaly. She felt now that, whether she liked him or not, he was helping Della, and was, therefore, a friend. And if he was to be a sort of friend, then she should help him.

She said now, "MacElvey wasn't lying when he said Yordy hates you and wants to kill you. I heard Miles tell him Yordy's proposition."

"That's old, and a lot of times it works," Chris observed idly.

"What is?"

"Warning a man he's in danger from someone else. It can cover a shot in the dark from anyone."

"Meaning Miles, in this case?" Kate asked quickly.

"That's who I meant."

They halted on the corner now before Melaven's, and Kate was shaking her head slowly. "I don't believe that. I'm not angry with you for saying it, but I don't believe it. It's just the way you are, the way you think."

A small frown creased Chris' forehead. He looked at her a long time before he said, "Where's Yordy? Let's ask him if he tried to sell Miles a way to kill me."

"Let's do," Kate said promptly, challengingly. "I'm

going to prove something either to myself or to you. He's at Briggs', south of town. Let's ride out. I'll be at the livery."

They parted without speaking and Kate, angry all over again, went straight for the livery stable. While she was waiting for her horse to be saddled, she suddenly realized that she was bareheaded and in street dress. It didn't matter. Some deep exasperation in her wouldn't let her turn back, wouldn't let her hesitate. Where, a few minutes before, she had wanted to help him, she was now out to prove for once and all that this silent, gray-eyed, gray-thinking man full of cynicism and hate, was wrong.

He had come into this country hating them all, more than eager to fight, and only chance had put him on the side of her friends. Yet even as he helped them, he was still eager for trouble, eager to believe nothing but what he saw and said himself. It was that infallibility of his that angered Kate now, that merciless judgment on people, friend or foe, of whom he knew nothing.

He was waiting in the street before the livery stable when she rode out and he put his horse in beside hers without a word. Kate noticed he carried his bandaged hand out of the way and high on his chest, hooking his little finger in the left pocket of his shirt.

When they were beyond the town, she mentioned it. "Your hand. Doesn't it bother you?"

"Yes."

There it is again, she thought. That maddening busi-

137

ness of speech, that iron self-sufficiency that needed nothing and gave nothing. She could almost hate him anew as she thought of it. She did not speak another word to him on the ride, and, being honest with herself, she thought he didn't care. *But he cared enough to ride out here to prove something,* she thought immediately afterwards, and pondered that until they approached Briggs' shack.

Yordy was out by a shed chopping wood as they rode up. He was shirtless and in his sock feet, and he was attacking the wood on the block with a kind of sullen fury.

The story was there for anyone to read it. Yordy had laid abed until early afternoon when hunger drove him to get up. There was no wood cut in this shiftless and shabby place, and Yordy, before he could eat, had had to cut some.

He didn't hear them until they were in the can-littered yard between him and the house. Then he turned suddenly, surprised, and Kate saw him recognize Danning and back up a pace and get a firm hold on his ax. They reined up before him and Yordy looked from Danning to Kate and back to Danning again. He was more puzzled than alarmed now.

He made a swipe with his free hand to smooth his awry hair, and said, "Hello, Miss Hardison. You lookin' for Joe?"

"No. You," Danning said. "I want to ask you a question." He paused, and Yordy's red-rimmed eyes became wary.

"Did you offer to sell Younger Miles a way to kill me?"

For a moment, Yordy didn't comprehend. Then, when he understood, he said hotly, promptly, "That's a lie! I never did, so help me God!"

There was more than a little fear in his answer, but his puzzlement had been genuine. Kate felt Chris' gray glance on her, and when she met his gaze he said, "That's not much proof. Is it enough?"

Kate looked at Yordy and said sternly, "Tell the truth, Frank. I sat beside Younger Miles this noon at the hotel and he told us—Mac, Truscott and me—that you'd offered to sell him a safe way to kill Danning. He even said he got it out of you what the way was. It was for him to put a man on top of that shale where the trail to the bench crosses it, and when Danning passed it would be easy to start a slide and bury him alive."

Yordy's jaw was sagging a little in amazement as Kate finished, and then the temper came. Only Kate's presence stopped the torrent of abuse that was in his face. A wild anger was in Yordy's loose face then, and there was something else besides anger. Whatever it was, Kate saw, it held Yordy silent, furious.

She heard Danning say then in a soft, derisive tone, "You've stayed here too long, Frank. Somebody— maybe me or Andy West or Leach Conover—is going to get shot at in the next couple of days. And MacElvey's coming straight for you on account of Miles' yarn. It's worked before."

Yordy's angry glance held Danning's unwaveringly for a full five seconds, and then a kind of startled expression came into his face.

"You've stayed too long," Chris repeated.

"I reckon I have," Yordy said bitterly, slowly. "But I'm goin'. And you can have Miles, Danning." He hesitated, almost uncertain, and then blurted out, "And you can have the right story of what I said to Miles, and be damned to his black heart!"

He told them then of his plan to get money and revenge on Danning and the Henhouse by selling Miles the suggestion of the fire. As he talked, angry and abject and defiant by turns, Kate felt a quiet despair. It was like turning over a loose board to expose the white nameless slugs under it to sight and then wanting to turn it back quickly, as instinct prompted. She wished she had not heard this, and she looked over at Danning.

He was listening attentively, his dark face impassive, as Yordy's story ended and she heard him say, "You better move, Frank, tonight, and keep to cover until you're out of the country."

Chris looked over now to Kate, ready to go. She pulled her horse around, not even wanting to look at Yordy again, and they rode off the place.

Kate did not speak for many minutes, and she was humble enough at the end of that time to say, "Well, I was wrong, and I'll admit it."

"But I was wrong, too," Chris replied thoughtfully. "Miles isn't going to bushwhack me. I misjudged him."

"Then you don't believe Yordy? You don't believe that's why Miles told that lie, to make Yordy guilty beforehand?"

Chris was quiet a long time, looking out over the flats, and finally he shook his head in negation and glanced over at her.

"You didn't like that back there, did you?"

"I hated it."

"You'll hate this worse. What I think. Do you want to hear it?"

Kate nodded in spite of her reluctance, watching him, and Chris said:

"Miles would have met him at Station, maybe paid him and ridden for the pass with him. But he would have shot him and left his body in the brush for somebody to find a week from now."

"Why do you say that?" Kate asked.

"Two reasons. He can't trust Yordy not to talk once the grass fire is set, no matter where Yordy is. The other reason is the main one. If Yordy was shot, it would stand to reason I shot him because he was trying to have me killed. With me out of the way in jail, and the grass fire over with, Della would quit."

Before she could answer, he said quietly, "I'll prove that, too. And to your father."

Kate said bitterly, "You'll have to, and to me too."

"I'll be on that porch at the hotel in Station, Sunday night. Let your father have a man—not MacElvey—in Station where he can see it. If Miles comes, can you doubt it?"

"You can doubt his intention to kill Yordy."

"But not his intention to pay Yordy off and see him out of the country, so he could burn the canyon."

Kate said softly, reluctantly, "No. I couldn't doubt that."

"Then tell him."

They were at the Coroner Canyon road now and Kate knew Chris would turn off to Box H. She reined up and so did he and raised his bandaged hand to touch his hat.

"You hate Younger Miles, don't you?" Kate said abruptly.

"Why—don't you?" Chris replied, surprised.

"But you knew this about him—his hatefulness. You already knew it."

Chris only touched his hat and said, "Good day," and rode off, but not before Kate had seen a sorrow mingled with that wild secret anger in his gray eyes.

Chapter X

Chris waited until Leach and Andy got up from the big Sunday dinner Della had prepared them and strolled off to their separate chores. Della relaxed in her chair and contemplated the table without much enthusiasm. Chris knew she missed her mother, and that cooking for three men was a lonely and confining job that chafed her spirit. He thought, too, that while she approved of their moving into Thessaly Canyon, she was afraid of what it might bring.

He finished his dinner slowly, eating clumsily with his left hand, his useless right hand in his lap. The nagging ache of it had never ceased, but he was used to it now and had banished it from his immediate awareness.

Della handed him the cigarette Andy had rolled for him and left in the middle of the table. He lighted it, and presently said, "Della, whose notion was it to hold those two-year-olds over this winter?"

"Yordy's, I guess," Della replied. "Why do you ask?"

"You're shipping them this fall," Chris said. "Miles could try that, but you can't risk it. You'll pour feed into them this winter, and they'll run off every pound of tallow you've bought them on the shipping drive. You're too far from a shipping point. Didn't Yordy know that?"

"But I've already borrowed money for feed and contracted for most of it," Della protested.

"Take what feed you have to, cancel what you can. Ship them this fall and pay back your money. Buy all the cows you can, because we'll have the grass. But leave the feeding to other people."

He could see the protest in Della's eyes.

"Do you know what prime three-year-olds will bring?" Della demanded, almost angrily.

Chris nodded. "Those are the three-year-olds you take half the summer to push sixty miles to a railroad. Over prairie in belly high grass. We've got a hundred and forty miles over a mountain range and two dry

143

drives to a railroad." He shoved back his chair, but before he rose he said, "I know, and you don't, Della, but it's your money. Which'll it be?"

Della's face had the sullen look of a scolded child's. "I'm not foolish enough to go against my foreman. We'll ship." She hesitated, and then added resentfully, "It's just the way you say things, Chris. You make a person want to say 'black' if you say 'white.'"

Chris rose and said indifferently, "I'm sorry, but that's my way."

"I know. But why is it?" Della said defiantly.

Chris regarded her closely, and then asked, "Sorry for your bargain, Della?"

"What makes you—" Della began defiantly, and then ceased talking and looked sullenly at Chris. "All right, I am, a little. This is no life, Chris. Mother's in town, and there are only three of you men and me against Miles. You've hurt his foreman, but he's got fifteen men left. What'll he do to us? We've moved in Thessaly. How will we hold it? What's going to happen?"

"Want to quit?"

"No, damn you, I don't!" Della flared, and then she flushed deeply, and presently she said with contrition in her tone, "I'm sorry, Chris. I'm not tired of my bargain, either. I suppose I'm just used to giving orders, not taking them." She looked at him and smiled faintly. "So are you."

Chris didn't answer and Della sighed, and then

stood up. Chris went out, then; he was puzzled and did not like this.

It was another cloudless day, with a hot ground wind stirring, and as he headed for the corral his rendezvous at Station tonight was already in his mind, Della out of it. It was of her cattle up there in Falls Canyon which was a ready fashioned weapon for Younger Miles. Younger wouldn't move until he was sure Yordy was safely out of the way, he thought, but he did not like to take the chance.

He caught his sorrel and spent long and laborious minutes left-handedly saddling him, and, as he worked, he came to his decision. The safest thing to do, even though Miles wouldn't move now, was to shove the beef out of the canyon today. But if he did that, some fiddle-footed Rainbow rider might see them or chance on the sign and report it to Miles who, knowing Yordy's plan was useless, would not bother to meet Yordy tonight. And Chris wanted Miles there tonight, had to have him. For he could then prove to Hardison's man and to all these people beyond any reasonable doubt that Miles wasn't simply a land-hungry man with a pretty wife and a solid place in the community, but a man who was a lawless killer. No, the cattle must stay there, then, but he could minimize the risk.

He led his sorrel over to the bunkhouse and stepped inside. Leach Conover was seated at the big table, mending bridle; he had the scraps already piled neatly, as if he wished to make as little mess as possible.

"Where's Andy?" Chris asked.

"Town," Leach said curtly. Since Chris' ultimatum, Leach hadn't bothered to hide his dislike of Chris. He did competently and slowly what he was ordered to do, and kept his counsel, even avoiding Andy when he could. It was as if Andy, by his decisive action at the shack that morning, had automatically stepped out of Leach's world of safe and friendly things, never to be readmitted.

Chris stood hesitant for a moment. He wanted Andy, because he knew Andy now, and he didn't know Leach. He silently berated himself for not having spoken to Andy before, but the harm was done.

"I've got a job for you, Leach," Chris said then. "Take your blankets and ride up to Falls Canyon this afternoon. I want you to camp there tonight, right at the brush fence. Don't make a fire, and sleep light. If anybody drifts up there, run 'em off."

Leach put down his punch. "Now that's the first time I ever heard Rainbow called cattle thieves, if that's what you mean."

"I don't. Just do what I said."

Leach picked up his punch and went to work again and Chris waited a moment for his assent, and when it did not come he said sharply, "Hear me, Leach?"

"I ain't deaf," Leach said sullenly.

Chris after a moment decided to let it go at that, and he went over to his bunk. His carbine in its scabbard hung on a nail in the wall, and he took it down and went out. He tied the scabbard to his saddle and mounted and rode out, and presently picked up the trail he and Andy had taken to the Bench. A kind of grim hopelessness touched him for a moment. Della's flare-up troubled him, and he knew that at last the reaction had set in. She had hired him on the whim of the moment, and when things had got rough and were on the verge of getting rougher, she hadn't much stomach for it. There was, Chris knew, little faith in her and little resolution, and he was glad she did not know of what Miles was planning for the Falls Canyon steers.

Once on the Bench, he took the trail pointed out to him yesterday by Andy which led through the climbing timber past a series of open parks to Falls Canyon and beyond. Once there, he surveyed the canyon briefly. Yordy had been right. The pine boughs of the temporary brush fence, itself only some forty yards in length across the narrow mouth of the box canyon, were brown from a summer's sun and tinder dry. The small stream which flowed under them trickled out of the deep sun-cured grass of the canyon which was mostly meadow and held only an occasional jackpine. A half dozen fat steers eating their way up the canyon stopped to watch him and then returned to grazing. Where they had trampled the grass, it was a thick brown mat; where they hadn't, their heads were lost to sight as they grazed it. The red sandstone walls of the canyon were deep and straight, making it the perfect trap Yordy had described.

Chris left the trail and cut west through the timber, and in late afternoon he came to the approaches to Thessaly Canyon. He was going to pay Tip Henry the call he had promised him.

He wondered what move Miles had made upon discovering Box H beef in the canyon. Coming out of the thinning timber, he found himself on the east rim close to the mouth. He pulled his horse close to the rim rock and looked about him, trying to locate himself.

The shack lay almost directly across the canyon from him, and the chuck wagon was gone, he saw. There were two saddled horses grazing, bridles slipped, in the grass on this side of the stream. A man and a woman were sitting on a log in the only spot of sun left in the clearing, and the man was not Tip Henry.

Chris recognized MacElvey immediately; his hat was off and his fiery hair was plain to see. It took him a little longer to recognize Abbie Miles, and when he did, he pondered this strange meeting here. It interested him only a moment, and then he put his horse along the rim and presently took a trail down into the canyon, speculating at the absence of Henry and the chuck wagon.

He rode aimlessly now, and when he was satisfied that the Box H beef was here and undisturbed, he turned back and followed the stream. Approaching the shack now, he saw only one horse grazing. Abbie Miles was sitting alone on the same log, her hat dangling idly by its chin strap from her fingers. She did not see him until her horse whickered.

Chris was close to her then, and he wanted the wagon road at the far edge of the clearing. He put his horse across the stream, and then touched his hat and said, "Afternoon, Mrs. Miles."

Abbie looked curiously at him and said, "Good afternoon, Mr. Danning. It is Mr. Danning, isn't it?"

Chris reined up and nodded, and said in a neutral voice, "It's a pleasant spot, isn't it?"

Abbie said dryly, with the faintest of smiles, "Ernie Coombs doesn't think so."

"He's a hard man to please," Chris murmured.

Abbie smiled openly then. "Are you going to finish the shack?"

"This is homestead land, and I am not the home-steader."

"Then you haven't heard," Abbie said, and laughed softly. Chris watched her, curious now.

"Tip has quit. He's afraid of you, Mr. Danning, so he asked for his time and rode out."

The import of this news came to Chris only a moment later, and he said gravely, "That won't please your husband, Mrs. Miles. Neither would your telling me about it."

"I very seldom please my husband," Abbie replied calmly, "or even try to."

Chris said then, "I have been meaning to ask you something, Mrs. Miles, but I haven't seen you. I wanted to ask your pardon for my discourtesy to you."

Abbie studied him in silence. He could tell she

knew he was referring to what he had said of her to Yordy there at Melaven's, and she seemed grateful that he had been no more specific. She nodded and said softly, "You are pardoned, although it was your right."

"That is no one's right," Chris said, and lifted his reins.

"You knew Younger before, didn't you?" Abbie said suddenly, and she was watching carefully for a sign of assent in his face.

"No, ma'am."

"I thought that might explain some things," Abbie said. "Good day, Mr. Danning."

As he touched his hat, Chris noticed for the first time the pair of saddlebags that lay at her feet. A flap of one was partly open; the necks of two bottles of whisky, grass stuffed between them, protruded.

Abbie saw his glance and looked down and fastened the flap, and then she said quietly, "It's still your right, you see, Mr. Danning."

"Good day," Chris said, and he rode on through the clearing to the wagon road.

So MacElvey was her source of whisky, Chris reflected; that accounted for the meeting he had witnessed earlier, and he thought closely of this. MacElvey's motive for supplying Abbie Miles with liquor baffled him, and he pondered it as he left the road and took the trail up the far side of the canyon.

In another hour he had put it out of his mind. It was twilight in the timber now and he rode steadily. He had been idling this afternoon, moving slowly in the direction of Station; now his pace was steady as he worked west. He chose each trail that would carry him into higher reaches of the Blackbows, and just before full dark he came out on the wagon road that led over the pass. He turned down it, knowing he was too high, and there was still light in the sky when he rode into Station.

A big two-story log house, its narrow veranda flush with the road, stood in a clearing across the road from a half dozen sagging barns and sheds. This was the old stage station antedating Triumph. The bar which was advertised by the weathered sign across the veranda reading HOTEL AND BAR, was patronized by almost every traveler too many miles from the next drink, and as Chris dismounted, the lamp in the bar was lighted.

The hotel, Chris guessed, was probably used only when the snow of the pass blocked travel. In the dusk, it had the color and appearance of an old and worn-out place quietly rotting away in the weather.

Taking his carbine from his boot, he speculated a moment as to whether he should hide his sorrel. Miles had told Yordy to have his stuff ready waiting. Miles, if there were no horse visible, might become suspicious and shy off, so that Hardison's man could not identify him.

Chris left the sorrel haltered to the veranda railing and climbed the sagging steps. He wondered if Hardison's man were here yet. The boards of the porch creaked as he crossed them, and before going into the bar he leaned his carbine against a weather-grayed chair by the door.

The bar across the rear wall was deserted, and the lamp on the bar top was smoking. The door that opened into the adjoining room was open, and Chris heard the sounds of a lamp being taken down and lighted.

He crossed to the bar and turned down the lamp-wick, and as he did so he heard the soft murmured "Thank you" of a woman's voice from the next room. The voice was oddly hushed, somehow familiar to him, but since this was unlikely, he dismissed it and leaned both elbows on the bar and scrubbed his cheek idly with the palm of his hand.

A man came into the room behind him, then, nudging the door half closed, and said, "Be right with you, son."

Bije Fulton was a fat and cheerless man who appeared as if he had been surprised halfway through dressing himself. His feet slapped softly in the pair of congress gaiters he wore, and his suspenders were trailing down behind his wide stern. He was too fat to wear a belt and his suspenders probably chafed his shoulders, Chris thought. He wore a collarless shirt of alternate red and white striped material, and his round and heavy face, needing a shave, had the fretful expression of a man who is too slow and knows it. He came around the bar and placed the lamp in its wall bracket and looked at Chris.

"Whisky," Chris said.

Bije put a bottle and glass in front of Chris and said, "Count your own drinks, two bits apiece. I got to eat."

He padded out the door in the back wall at the end of the bar and Chris poured his drink and downed it.

He heard the door behind him swing open, and looked over his shoulder, and there was Kate Hardison. The glass was still in his hand. He put it down and walked over to her and said, "Why did they bring you up here?"

"I came by myself," Kate said.

"Your father sent you?"

"Who else was there to send?"

Kate's question held him silent. Whom had he expected? One of the commissioners who was either a friend of Miles or business partner, and who could not be trusted not to tip off Miles beforehand? Or a townsman awed by Miles' power and money?

Kate said then, "Walt said I'd seen part of it, even started part of it. It was up to me to see it through."

A woman! Chris thought grimly, and then immediately, *Why not?* He looked beyond her into the bar parlor and said, "You'll have to stay in there, with the lamp out."

"I've got a room upstairs. I can see the road and hear him too. I'll go up there."

Chris nodded assent. She was to be trusted, and that's all he really cared about. There was one more thing he wanted to make sure of, and he asked, "What about the fat man?"

"Bije? He's his own man."

Kate was wearing a dark riding habit with divided skirt, which made her look even slighter than usual. A momentary curiosity stirred in Chris now. She didn't like this, didn't want to believe it, didn't want to be here, and yet she had come. Some of the friendliness he felt for her at that moment must have been communicated to Kate, for she smiled faintly and said, "I can give you some advice if you're going to sit on the veranda and wait for him. Cover your bandage. He can see it in the dark."

She turned then and left him, and Chris tramped thoughtfully to the porch and got his jumper that was tied behind his saddle. That was good advice, but why did she care?

He came back to the porch and pulled the chair away from the door, placing it in deep black shadow, and sat down. Leaning his carbine against the wall beside him, he relaxed in his chair, first wrapping the jumper about his bandage.

It was full dark now and the lamp threw an oblong of light down the steps and into the dust. Across the way in the corral a pair of horses quarreled and squealed and were silent again, and the silence of the night settled. Chris turned his head away from the lamplight so that his eyes would adjust themselves to the darkness. He was ready, and Hardison's witness was ready. Chris anticipated this with a slow and wicked relish, for up to now he had been patient, placing Della's welfare ahead of his own business, as he had promised. This now was his own personal affair; his obligations had been served.

The fat man, Bije, rattled the stove somewhere deep in the house, and on the heel of this noise Chris heard the first faint dust-muffled footfalls of a horse approaching from down the road. He reached for his carbine and laid it across the arms of his chair, the butt to the left side, for it would be from the left side he must shoot if trouble came.

A rider presently loomed indistinctly in the darkness, black against the gray of the road. He came on a ways and reined up, as if surveying the building, and Chris thought, *He's looking to see if Yordy's set to go,* and he came out of his chair and stepped back against the wall as the rider put his horse in motion again. The rider came boldly on and then, some thirty feet from the veranda, he reined up and his voice came quietly, "That you, Frank?"

It was Younger Miles speaking.

Chris said softly, "Frank couldn't come," and watched Miles' body stiffen to attention in the saddle.

"Who's that? Speak up!" Miles said sharply.

"Yordy's run out on you, Miles," Chris said. "Anything you'd like to take up with me about Falls Canyon?" He moved slowly to one side as he finished.

The swiftness of the shot surprised him. He heard the slug smash into the chair, and as he raised his carbine he thought: *He had his gun in his hand waiting for Yordy to answer.*

He shot too soon, clumsily, getting no real sight from his left shoulder, and already Miles had shot again. Chris' shot hit; he heard it, and then Miles' horse screamed. Miles' third shot boomed into the veranda roof and then Chris heard the heavy earth-shaking sound of Miles' horse going down, while he was trying savagely and clumsily to lever a shell into his carbine with his left hand. He could not, and the sense of urgency was wild within him. He looked up and saw Miles come to his knees in the oblong of lamplit dust where his horse had pitched him as it went down. Miles crawled on his knees now, frantically beating the dust for the gun he had dropped.

Chris forgot his carbine then. He put his hand out on the rail to vault it and only when his weight was in motion did he realize he had used his injured hand to support himself. The savage racking pain of it shocked up his shoulder and he tried to take the weight from his hand and his body crashed into the rail. A tearing sound of wood accompanied his fall as the rail gave way. He landed heavily on his side in the road, his carbine still in his hand. Coming to his knees, trying desperately, awkwardly to lever in the shell, he saw Miles rise, in the shaft of light from the saloon lamp. His hands were empty. He looked once, his face twisted with fury, in Chris' direction and heard the shell in Chris' carbine finally slip home. He ran, then, out into the night. Chris lifted his gun, sighting through the shaft of light, and he could see nothing, and rose to his feet, running, too, and crossed the lamplit oblong of ground.

The touch of light had destroyed his vision too.

Cursing, he halted and raised his gun. He had to rest the gun on the back of his right wrist, and even as he shot at the sound of Miles' running rather than at his dim, blurred figure, he knew it was useless. He ran on, now, and he heard Kate's sharp cry, "Chris! Chris!" from the porch and paid it no attention, concentrating now on the fumbling way he was levering in another cartridge as he ran.

Rounding the corner of a shed, he halted, listening. Off in the timber now, he heard the crashing of brush, and behind that sound the swift pounding of Kate running toward him. He raised his gun again and lowered it, and a great sigh of disappointment came from him.

Kate reached him now and grabbed his arm and swung him around with the slight weight of her.

"Chris, don't follow him!" Kate begged.

The wild voice of Miles came from the timber then. "Next time I'll hold onto my gun, Danning!"

Chris half started for him, and then hauled up and looked bleakly at the carbine in his hand. He heard Kate say from beside him, "Are you hit?"

"No. Neither is he," Chris said bitterly. He looked at her now, and she let go his arm. "Are you sure of it now?" he asked in the same bitter voice. "He had the gun in his hand, waiting for Yordy to sing out."

"I know, I know," Kate said gently. "I believe you."

They regarded each other in the darkness for a moment, and then Chris turned back, and Kate fell in beside him.

The rage was still in him, but it was a rage at himself. He had let Miles surprise him, and that was stupid. He should have trusted his ability to handle his six-gun lefthanded. If his one lucky shot hadn't hit Miles' horse and pitched both him and his gun into the dust, he would have been cornered. His hand throbbed with every beat of his heart and he lifted it against his chest, the pain of it driving all else from his mind.

Kate halted in the oblong of lamplight. It was not an unfilled oblong now, for Bije Fulton stood framed in the doorway behind.

"Who's shootin'?" he demanded.

"Put a light on this dead horse out here and you'll know," Kate answered tartly.

When she turned to look up at Chris the fear and the worry in her face had not yet vanished. "I think we both ought to see Walt now. Are you coming with me?"

Chris thought of that, and he knew, fool or not, he'd proved his point tonight. He said, "Yes," and looked longingly back at the timber.

Younger stood at the edge of the timber until Kate and Danning had ridden out, and still he stood there, in the grip of angry indecision. He had made one serious mistake tonight, and he did not want to make another one by moving too soon.

Yordy, of course, had sold him out, and in discovering it he had lost his head and shot at Danning. The whole setup was plain to him now. Kate Hardison had been placed where she could hear him and see him, and she would carry her tale of how he had planned to kill Yordy back to town and use it against him. That much was certain; that much was serious, because if she hadn't had the whole story from Yordy, she wouldn't have been here.

He saw Bije come out of the barroom carrying a lantern, and walk over to the downed horse. Bije would identify it and corroborate Kate's story. *It can't be helped,* he thought grimly, and left the timber, walking slowly toward the hotel.

The whole way of his life here would be changed now, he thought soberly, and his recklessness tonight was responsible. He thought narrowly then of what it would mean to him materially, and he decided it would not mean much. If he got the Sulinam mines contract tomorrow, he could buy out the town. Even if he didn't, Truscott was involved with the bank's money and his own money in so many affairs with Miles that he couldn't afford to lift a finger against him. No, his money and investments were safe. It was the intangible things, though, the slow accretion of respect from people, the chance of a lawful acquisition of power that he had lost forever tonight, and, thinking of this, he hated Danning with a murderous passion. He thought again now, *What does he want? Who is he?*

Bije, lantern held high over his head, was still regarding the horse. He heard Miles' approach and lowered the lantern and looked in Miles' direction.

When he recognized him, Bije grunted. He gestured

helplessly to the horse, and said, "He's dead. What do you want done with him?"

"Anything you damn please," Younger said flatly. "I want a horse, Bije. I'll send him back tomorrow."

"All right," Bije said. "Only, look. If you and him was fightin' over her, she don't come here any more. You tell her I run a decent place."

Younger swore at him then, and Bije, not much surprised, put the lantern down and said, "Get your own damn horse, you sorehead," and tramped slowly into the barroom.

Younger got his saddle off his dead black, picked up the lantern, and went over to the corral. There was a bay and a chestnut inside, and he caught and saddled the bay, afterwards blowing out Bije's lamp and hanging it on the corral pole.

Stepping into the saddle, he still did not spur his horse, but sat there motionless. Again he speculated on the probable effect of tonight's happenings when news of it got out, and again he could not see how he could come out of it with his reputation unhurt. Oddly, now, he remembered Danning's words to O'Hea that Mac had repeated: "Tell him to work it rough and in the open. He knows how."

He touched spurs to his horse now, heading down the canyon for Rainbow. Yes, he knew how, and he would work it rough. And soon.

160

Chapter XI

Yordy's fright was pretty well gone by the time he was deep in timber. He'd spent most of Saturday night drinking with Joe Briggs and giving mysterious reasons for his sudden exodus, meanwhile haggling interminably over the sale of his string of horses and his effects, which were still at the hotel and which Joe had never seen and did not really want to buy.

They came to an agreement a couple hours before dawn and Yordy took Joe's one hundred and forty dollars and rode out, swaying in the saddle, a propertyless man.

He reached the foothills east of Box H at midmorning, Sunday. Following the old logging road which was Box H's east boundary, noon found him in the foothills, sober, half sick and in need of sleep. He pulled off the road and slept for a couple of hours, and in midafternoon began his journey again and presently reached timber.

The urgency of his departure, now that he was sober, seemed exaggerated, and he was acutely aware that in some indefinable way he had been swindled. A few days ago he had had a job, a steady salary, four good horses and the clutter of stuff, some of it valuable, that any man collects. A few days after that, he had all this and the promise of five hundred dollars, too. And now, at the moment, he had his horse, and the clothes on his back, the few in his bedroll, his gun, and one hundred and forty dollars. It was a sorry showing for five years of sweat and toil, he concluded.

When night came, he made his lonely camp off the logging road, and to demonstrate to himself his contempt for danger, and his desperation, he boldly built a big fire and cooked his grub. Afterwards, over a bitter cigar that must have been dry the day it was made, he gave himself over to self-pity and recrimination. With any luck at all, he might now be sitting on the porch at Station waiting for Miles to hand him his five hundred dollars.

Between cursing himself for his cowardice and justifying it to himself, he finally concluded that the two Harms women at Henhouse were basically responsible for his position now. Danning was directly responsible, he supposed, but Della had thrown over her foreman of five years for this tough stranger.

He threw away his cigar and lay down, wishing savagely that Miles might have paid him the money, fired the canyon, and then been caught. It would have paid Miles off in the coin he deserved, and it would have paid the Harms women off, too. He was idly studying the gloomy pattern the pines made against the star glitter when the thought hit him.

He sat bolt upright, and for long minutes he calculated the risks. Hell, there weren't any—or if there were, he'd soon know, and in time to run.

Swiftly now, he set about breaking camp. He lashed up his bedroll, caught and saddled his horse which was close on picket, and stamped out his fire. Mounting, he backtracked a ways and found the trail that took him west into the heart of Box H range. The stars said it was close to ten o'clock when he looked at them now.

Leach was watching those same stars, and he had been doing so for a sleepless hour. The cold biscuits and steaks he had eaten tonight in deference to Danning's request not to build a fire sat like a handful of river pebbles in his stomach. When it came time to make up his bed tonight, he had discovered that all the pine trees handy had had their lower branches lopped off months ago to build the brush fence beside him. He had no ax and it was dark, so he could not cut pine boughs for his bed, and he had rolled up in his blanket in the grass.

Each small hump gouged his old bones, and Leach lay sleepless, imagining endless tomorrows of stiffness and perhaps rheumatism. He was too old for this kind of thing—under the kind of foreman the Harms women now had. A troublemaker and a driver, Danning was, suspecting trouble where it didn't exist. Did anyone who knew this country and its people think for a moment that Younger Miles or any Rainbow hand was going to steal these cattle? Where would he hide them, after he'd left a trail for a blind man to read?

Sleep would not come. The thought of the bunkhouse, with a level bunk and a soft hay-filled mattress, tormented him for minutes on end. A smoke might help, he thought, and he was already sitting up reaching for the sack of dust in his shirt pocket when he remembered Danning's injunction: No fire. He cursed bitterly and lay back on his saddle, which, covered with his jumper, made his unsatisfactory pillow. A simmering, crochety resentment came over him now. It was a fact: when you got old, you were discarded—unless you stuck up for your rights.

Leach fanned his anger by naming those rights over in his mind, and in the midst of naming them, he felt the thing run over his blankets. He jumped out of his blankets, fighting blindly to get away from whatever it was. Then he calmed down and swore bitterly.

Probably only a mouse. But dammit, if he'd been allowed to build a fire, which would have kept things away from him, and been allowed to get some sleep so he wouldn't know if they ran over his blanket or not, he wouldn't be this jumpy.

That does it! he thought savagely. He stood there, mad, fed up, mutinous. The thought of the long ride back to the bunkhouse wasn't inviting. And then he thought of the line shack back in the Salt Meadow a quarter mile below. The shack had a bunk and a roof and a stove, and he could hear the bawling of any cattle that anybody tried to run out of Falls Canyon tonight in time to do something about it.

He scrambled around in the dark for his gear, his decision reinforced by the new difficulty of finding his stuff in the dark. Finally, he rolled his blankets and lugged his saddle down to his horse, mounted, and rode off. He was mad at himself now for not having thought of the shack sooner.

Yordy approached the canyon by the upper trail around the rim. He rode without any special caution, since he could explain his presence here to anybody except Miles, and Miles was sitting on the porch at Station waiting for him, he hoped. Coming down the steep trail that let out onto the flat at the mouth of the canyon, he turned toward the brush fence.

When he came to where the fence should be, he dismounted and walked over and felt the dry brush of it crackle under foot. He moved toward the creek and clear across the canyon, and then returned, satisfied the brush fence was still unbroken. If the cattle had been moved, the fence wouldn't have been replaced.

He paused a moment now, tasting the perfection of his plan. Danning would swear Miles did it and Miles would deny it. If they were both so anxious to fight, there was the opportunity. And the Harms women could work out that loan from the bank for as long as they cared to. It would still be there years from now.

He lighted his match and touched it to the dry brush. The flame guttered indecisively only a moment and then caught, and the dry needles burned with almost explosive force.

Yordy was so surprised at the violence of the fire that he was panicked for a moment, and moved to his horse. He mounted and watched the fire move swiftly along the piled brush, its flames a good ten feet high. Before it all caught, the grass of the canyon behind it started to burn with a sharp dry crackle, shooting sparks into the night.

Satisfied, Yordy put his horse up the trail and, from a vantage point close to the rim, he watched it take hold and spread. The sun-cured grass of last season underneath the dry stuff of this year burned savagely, popping and shooting sparks like exploding coals. A solid wall of flame, five and six feet high, moved slowly up the canyon, fed by the natural draft of warm air from the flats moving up through the timber and up the canyon.

When it was alight from canyon wall to canyon wall, a great shaft of sparks rose into the night. Yordy had wanted to see it trap the cattle, but now he was frightened of what he had started. This might turn into a forest fire if some of these drifting sparks landed in the right place, he thought. If that were the case, he wanted to be over the mountains, and he rode purposefully for the creek above the falls, where he could pick up a trail over the peaks.

The fire burned slowly, thoroughly. Where it held back in one place for a tree, breaking the line of flame, it soon caught on again on the other side and the ragged line of flame marched on unbroken. The cattle moved away from it, at first slowly, then, as they saw each other and spread the panic among themselves, more swiftly, pausing occasionally to turn and stare at it.

It took a long time for the noise of the fire to penetrate Leach's consciousness. When it did, he dressed and rode up to the canyon, and the fire by now was three quarters of the distance from the mouth. Leach's horse balked at approaching the first dead steer. Leach fought him halfheartedly, for the smoke and ashes were making him cough. He moved back into an elder thicket and got a drink, holding carefully to the reins of his horse, and before he mounted he stood motionless, thinking of the implications of this.

He never told me it was fire he was afraid of or I'd have stayed, Leach thought bleakly. That satisfied him and justified his action in his own mind, but he knew behind the thought that he'd have to leave now. He could never work for Danning after this.

Toward the upper end, he started coming across the cattle. They were scattered in pairs or singly among the glowing coals in the fire's wake. He rode on among them, coughing, and when he saw that not one steer remained alive, he turned and followed the creek out of the canyon.

Chapter XII

There was a lamp alight in the house when Younger got back from Station, but the bunkhouse was dark. Nevertheless, after he turned Bije's horse into the corral, Younger went over to the bunkhouse and woke

Ernie and, squatting beside his bunk in the darkness, told him of the fight with Danning. Tomorrow, Younger said, he wanted Ernie to take three or four of the crew into town early. If trouble came, over what had happened tonight, they would be ready.

Learning that O'Hea was over at the house with Mrs. Miles, Younger said good night and stepped out into the darkness, heading for the house. O'Hea's horse was tied to the picket fence enclosing the yard. As he went through the gate, Younger heard, over the clamor of the rushing Coroner, the sound of his wife playing the piano, and he thought, *That damned racket tonight, of all nights.*

Entering the kitchen, he was reminded of his hunger. He pocketed a handful of cookies, put one in his mouth, and went on into the dining room. Abbie was playing softly, absently at the grand piano in the living room; O'Hea, head back and eyes closed, sat in a chair beside her listening. Miles tramped in and said around the cookie, "Hullo, O'Hea. Good thing you came tonight."

Abbie ceased playing. O'Hea reluctantly sat up and took a last look around this tasteful room, as if he knew the peace would soon go out of it.

Younger looked at Abbie now, and noted the unnatural flush of her cheeks and the brightness of her eyes, and a hot disgust rose in him. "Boozing again?" he asked.

Abbie didn't answer him; her face only grew a little sullen.

Younger said disgustedly to O'Hea, "Since when did you sit around watching her pour booze into herself?"

"She can do what she wants," O'Hea said tiredly. "She's grown up."

Younger crammed another cookie in his mouth and rubbed his sugared hand across his coat. Dragging a heavy rocker across the rug he sat down in it, facing O'Hea.

"You're feeling better, O'Hea. Did you know it? Well enough to take up your duties again." The heavy irony of his voice was undisguised. He chewed on his cookie, completely unself-conscious.

"Now what?" Abbie asked cynically.

"I'm in trouble, kind of," Younger said, not looking at her. "I had a tangle with Danning tonight. I may get scolded for it tomorrow, and I want you back in office. They can kick Mac out as not elected, but they can't kick you out."

"What kind of a tangle?" Abbie asked.

Younger put another cookie in his mouth and told them. It was an artless telling of it, as if they, like Ernie, would be disinterested in the ethics of what he was relating. But he did not tell what fate he had planned for Yordy at Station. He had underestimated Danning, he said, but that was only incidental. He wanted everything in order, so that if his denial were disbelieved, there was still nothing anybody could do about it.

"You think they'll believe your story?" Abbie asked.

"Likely not. I don't care."

"Since when don't you care?" Abbie asked dryly.

Younger looked fully at her for the first time. "Since tonight. After it wouldn't do any good to care. I'm a practical man."

"But not so practical you'd take my advice about leaving Yordy alone."

Younger's hooded dark eyes regarded her for three long seconds and then he said, "I had to take a chance on Yordy. I'll take any chance, so long as I can run Danning out of here. And I'll run him out."

"I don't think you will," Abbie said slowly. "I met him today. I don't think you will."

"You met him?" Younger asked. "Where?"

"Up at Tip's shack. I rode up there."

"What was he doing up there?" Younger asked, alarmed now. "Taking over?"

"No, I asked him if he was, and he said no."

"You asked him if he was?" Younger said slowly. "How did he know Tip was gone? How did he know he could take it?"

Abbie, too late, realized that she had betrayed herself. It was true she had been drinking, and now the drink had died in her she was tired and sleepy and her mind not quick. She thought now of her brave verbal defiance of Younger to Danning today and it gave her a sudden and real defiance.

"How did he?" Younger repeated, and came to his feet.

"I told him," Abbie said.

Younger's reaction was instinctive. He slapped her

heavily across the mouth, and when she cried out and shrank back on the piano stool, he raised his hand again, but let it fall in a kind of angry bafflement and contempt.

He looked hotly at O'Hea, who had not moved. "There's your daughter, man! Sells her husband out with a smile. I could have bluffed Danning about Tip, and for six months I could have held that shack and used it, and fenced that canyon against him."

He looked down at Abbie, who was crying quietly, her head bent.

"If you can't be for me, then keep your drunken mouth shut!" he said in a cold anger.

He looked now at O'Hea, and the sight of him seemed to anger him further. "Just once, so help me, I wish I could say either one of you did one thing right. Just once."

He glared at O'Hea and then, seeing that he could not even provoke a protest, he said, "Ah-h!" in a fathomless disgust and started for the kitchen. Remembering his original errand now, he paused and said to O'Hea, "Bright and early in your office, O'Hea. And have your letter written."

He went out and they heard the kitchen door slam.

Presently, O'Hea rose and went over to Abbie and put his hand on her shoulder and patted it. He took a turn around the room, staring unseeing at each picture on the wall as he passed it, and then he was back at his chair. He sank into it and said, "That happened before, Abbie?"

171

"It's the first time," Abbie said.

O'Hea stared at the pattern of the rug, not seeing it. The whole sorry history of these past few years was parading across his mind. It had started with his wife's death eight years ago, out on the ranch. Before he'd really found his bearings again after that, the bad winter of the next year had smashed him. The outfits close to the Blackbows hadn't suffered so much, but his place out on the flats to the north had been wiped clean of stock by the succession of blizzards—stock that was bought on borrowed money. He'd been forced to work for other outfits, then, putting Abbie in town with friends, but even that didn't last after his health began to fail. His old friends had backed him for sheriff then, and he'd won the office and its small salary, which Abbie supplemented by working at the hotel.

She was still working there when Younger met and courted and married her. O'Hea wondered now, with a passive bitterness, why he had ever thought they were badly off in the old days. He had his pride then, and a remnant of health and manhood left him, and he would have killed the man who laid a hand on Abbie. But a moment ago he had sat here and done nothing when Miles hit her. A scalding shame flooded him and he looked over at Abbie.

"You fed up as I am, Abbie?"

Abbie only nodded.

O'Hea stood up and his tone when he spoke was humble, soft. "You've stayed on my account, haven't

172

you? You figured a sick old man was entitled to lie comfortable in the sun after he was through, didn't you? Well, so did I, maybe, and maybe I was worried about who'd take care of you."

Abbie didn't answer and O'Hea held out his hand and looked at it. It was trembling; it had never ceased trembling. He hid it in his pocket and said with a soft stubborn gentleness, "I'm goin' to fight him, Abbie. I've made up my mind. I'd rather die fightin' him than live this way."

Abbie looked up quickly, and she and her father regarded each other with unfaltering gaze. "We used to make out when I was at the hotel. We can again," Abbie said swiftly.

O'Hea shook his head. "Don't go back on my account, Abbie."

"Then on my own!" Abbie said quickly, passionately. "Oh Dad, think of it! We don't need much, and together we can make out. If you'll fight him, I'll leave him. I'll never want to take another drink, even."

She came into his arms then, and he held her tight to him, neither of them saying anything.

O'Hea kissed her then and went out into the hall and got his hat. Abbie opened the front door, and O'Hea halted and regarded her fondly. "You're too fine a girl to drink."

Chapter XIII

Leach stopped at the house first and wakened Della. They talked for a while, and by that time dawn was breaking. Leach came over to the bunkhouse and lighted the lamp, waking both Chris and Andy.

He stood in the middle of the floor and said sourly, "Della wants to see you both," and walked out.

When he was gone, Andy climbed out of his bunk and looked sleepily at Chris. "What's this?"

Chris didn't know and said so. They dressed rapidly and in silence, and walked together through the fading night toward the lamplit house.

Leach was seated in the kitchen at the table where Della sat, too, and a tall-chimneyed, shadeless lamp sat on the table between them. Della wore a belted wrapper and her brown hair was loose, cascading down over her shoulders. She sat sideways in her chair and her back was to the wall, one arm thrown over the back of the chair. Her face was cold and unfriendly and Chris, seeing it, had a premonition of trouble.

Andy dragged a chair against the sidewall and sat down, and put both big hands on his knees in an attitude of patient expectancy.

Chris stood by the other chair, and when Della saw he wasn't going to sit down she said, "Falls Canyon was fired last night, Chris. Every steer lost."

A sick and dismal feeling hit Chris like a blow, then, and he said nothing, thinking nothing. Della watched him without any friendliness about her now, and presently she said, "It happened before midnight, Leach said."

Chris shuttled his gaze to Leach, who sat taciturnly in the corner, an arm on the table. "Where were you?" Chris asked him.

"He was sleeping in the line shack at the Salt Meadow," Della said quietly. "He's not to blame, Chris. You didn't even bother to tell him it was fire you were afraid of. He thought you were afraid of the cattle being driven off, and he could have heard that at the shack."

Chris didn't say anything; he only looked at Leach, thinking *I should have known,* and his eyes were hard and unforgiving.

"You were afraid of fire, weren't you?" Della went on.

Chris only nodded.

"Then if you were afraid of it, you knew somebody planned it. We didn't. I didn't. Did you, Andy?"

Andy cleared his throat and crossed his legs and said, "Yes, ma'm."

Chris looked swiftly at him and then said, "Andy didn't either. Thanks, Andy."

Andy cleared his throat again and said nothing.

"Why didn't you tell us?" Della asked relentlessly.

"I should have, maybe, but it was my responsibility."

"And you turned it over to Leach."

"He knew what to do," Chris said quietly.

175

"You never told me it was fire you was afraid of, or I'd of stayed," Leach said flatly.

"Are you blaming Leach?" Della asked, and now she could not keep the anger from her voice.

"Yes, ma'm," Andy put in calmly.

"No," Chris said.

There was a long silence now, and Della's face was still unfriendly, still strained with a dislike of him she could hide no longer, Chris saw.

"If you knew somebody planned it, maybe you'll tell me who it was—now that the cattle are dead. About six thousand dollars worth of beef, if you'll allow me to mention it."

Chris told them then of how pure chance, the result of his argument with Kate Hardison over the truth of Miles' story, took them to Briggs' place, and of Yordy's subsequent confession. He told also of the inconclusive fight last night, and the reasons for his wanting to leave the beef, guarded by Leach, in the canyon, so as not to alarm Miles and risk missing him. His reasons for each move still seemed sound to him as he talked, although he did not take the trouble to justify himself.

When he had finished, Della said, "So Younger Miles did it?"

"Not if Leach was right about the time. It was Yordy."

"Ah," Della said, with a small malice. "You didn't think of Yordy, did you, while you were watching Miles?"

176

"He put Leach there, didn't he?" Andy asked softly.

Temper flared in Della's violet eyes now as she looked at Andy, and he received her look placidly, his eyes steady.

Della's glance shifted to Chris, and he said gently, then, "Mother was right, wasn't she, Della?"

For a moment he thought Della was going to pretend ignorance of his meaning, and then she nodded slowly. "Yes, mother was right about you. You're not our stripe, are you?"

Chris shook his head in negation.

"The day I hired you, I told you Box H was all mother and I had, and that you had to put it first."

"And I did."

"Do you call it putting us first when you lost us six thousand dollars just so you could prove your point about Younger?"

"Leach was there," Andy repeated stubbornly.

"Stop saying that, Andy!" Della said sharply. "It wasn't Leach's fault."

"It was, too," Andy said, unruffled. "Seems to me you're sorry for your bargain, so you're blamin' Chris."

"Why shouldn't I be sorry?" Della demanded hotly. "All he's brought us is trouble."

"And Thessaly Canyon," Chris said dryly. "Your cattle are there. Tip Henry's quit the country, and his homestead's void. You've got your old range."

Della only shook her head, her face sullen and determined. Nobody spoke. Chris noticed in the silence that day was here. The lamp burned brightly on the table and nobody made a move to blow it out.

Chris said then, "You want me to go, Della?"

"Yes. I wish you'd go away. I wish you'd never come. Maybe when you're gone, Leach and Andy and I can figure some way to pay off that note without the beef money. We can't with you here."

Andy stood up now. "You and Leach, maybe, but not me."

"Just as you like," Della said, coldly. "All you've got to do to quit is walk in and ask Truscott for your time."

"Yes, ma'm," Andy said.

Chris turned and went out now, into the morning, and Andy followed him. Under the big cottonwood, Chris halted and Andy halted too, looking at him expectantly.

"You stay, Andy," Chris said. "She needs you."

"Not me and Leach both, she don't," Andy said stubbornly.

"Mrs. Harms will come back. That will be three women."

Andy's placid face broke a little and he smiled, and a faint gleam of humor and friendliness was in Chris' eyes, too. They understood each other completely in that moment. Andy didn't have to say that he thought an injustice had been done to a friend, and that because he was finally his own man, he could quit in protest. Nor did Chris have to say that Della was scared, and that she needed help now, beyond all other times. All that was understood without needing speech, and Andy said quietly, "I'll get your horses."

Chris went into the bunkhouse and with his clumsy left hand lashed his few belongings in his blankets. Oddly, he felt a sense of relief now, and he thought, *I can get on with it now. I haven't got her to worry about.*

He slung his bedroll and his pack over his shoulder and stood in the doorway of the bunkhouse a moment, looking over this pleasant place. An unaccountable regret touched him; he had mixed in the lives of these people only reluctantly, and yet they were a part of him now, and he would remember them. He did not like that; he had room for only one thought and one purpose, and as he tramped over to the corral he was already trying to put them and this from his mind. But he knew immediately that he couldn't forget Andy, because Andy had risked something for him; nor Della, who had no faith.

Andy had the sorrel saddled, and now he put the pack on Chris' short-coupled pack horse. There came the moment when he was ready to go, and Andy, seeing it, said, "Well," and hesitated, looking at Chris. "Drifting?"

"That's about it, Andy."

"Good luck," Andy said. "You've earned some."

"Luck yourself," Chris said. "Make up for Leach."

There was no way to shake hands, so they didn't. Chris mounted and Andy handed him the lead rope of his pack horse and stood back. Chris rode out past the bunkhouse, and as he approached the cottonwood Della came out of the house.

She had dressed and done up her hair, but as he reined up, Chris noticed her face hadn't changed its reflection of her determination to do an unpleasant duty.

"I didn't mean to send you off without breakfast, Chris. Stay for that."

"It's better this way," Chris said mildly.

"Not all people are as tough as you, Chris," Della said, accusingly, and she stepped back. "Good luck."

"Shall I tell your mother Leach will be in after her this morning?"

Della nodded. "If you will."

Chris touched his hat with his bandaged hand and rode out, and Della stood looking at his high shoulders and straight back. He didn't turn around, and presently, the morning now bright, she went slowly into the house.

Chris did look back, once he was atop the bald hill, and a gray bitterness was in him. Della's cowardice had isolated him, cutting off any expectancy of help, or even shelter, from anyone. Her defeat was his own, and his legal weapon for wrecking Miles was gone, now that Box H had quit fighting. He was as alone now as the night he had ridden in, save for Hardison's feeble help. Then he faced ahead, and already his mind was shaping up the only thing that was left him, and he thought *I can kill him now.*

Chapter XIV

Younger rode into Triumph at his usual time, left his horse at the livery and crossed the street to the store. He saw Ernie Coombs, his bandaged hand white and big at this distance, yarning with someone in front of Melaven's. Younger went into his store and on through to the office where Mac, in shirt-sleeves, was already at work.

Mac returned his greeting and then leaned back in his chair and said over his shoulder, "Walt Hardison wanted to see you as soon as you came in."

Younger grinned faintly at that and took up his hat again. "You might like to come with me, Mac."

"I know," MacElvey said, "I'm invited, too." He smiled faintly. "Have you been breaking the law?"

"I was shot at," Younger said sardonically, "so somebody must have broken it."

Then went out together, and instead of crossing immediately to the hotel Younger kept to the board-walk until he met Ernie.

"Go pick up O'Hea, Ernie," Younger directed. "Bring him over to Hardison's."

"He's there, now," Ernie murmured. "Truscott too. Just went in. Want me?"

Younger grunted a negative and swung into the street. Hardison wasn't losing any time. That was all right, too, Younger thought grimly. It would take only a very few minutes for him to state his case, which he had built into a reasonable one, and they could take it or leave it. He was, as a matter of fact, less interested about his story being believed than he was in the outcome of the Sulinam bid, news of which he would receive today. Before he entered the hotel, he identified Bill Arnold and Stew Shallis loafing about the street, and knew Ernie had done his job.

Nobody was behind the desk, and Younger led the way up the stairs and knocked once on the parlor door and was bid to enter. Hardison was propped up on the pallet underneath the window that opened onto the veranda, his back to the wall. Younger wondered irrelevantly what Hardison's legs looked like, and if they were shriveled as he had heard they were.

He said, "Morning, gentlemen," in a bold voice and nodded to Truscott and Hardison. He gave O'Hea a sharp and searching glance and looked about the room for a chair. There was something about his bull-like arrogance and size then that O'Hea quietly marveled at, and O'Hea watched him with a curious tranquility in his sick eyes.

While Mac took the closest chair, Younger sat down slowly in the big armchair across the room and, taking a cigar from his pocket, looked quizzically around the room. "You look awful damn solemn for this early hour, gentlemen. What's this about?"

Walt said mildly, "Kate's comin' up. We'll wait for her."

Younger nodded complacently and lighted his cigar.

He had just got it going well when Kate stepped into the room and closed the door behind her. She wore a full blue skirt, a lighter-colored blouse of blue, too, and Younger, observing her as she smiled faintly at Walt and sat down in the chair beside him, thought her a handsome little shrew.

Walt said to Truscott, "I called you over, John, to hear something Kate told me. You, Sam and Mac, can listen and reflect. . . . Go ahead, Kate."

It was that simple, and Kate began it with Miles' story related in the dining room in her presence; and Truscott, listening impassively, nodded. She went on to her meeting with Danning in MacElvey's office, and of their subsequent argument as to the authenticity of Miles' story. Miles listened carefully, the cigar clenched tightly in his teeth, while Kate told of Danning's and her visit to Yordy, and of Yordy's confession.

She went on from there, telling of what happened the previous night at Station, and Younger leaned forward as she talked, a calculated bafflement and protest in his face. It was a damning story, he admitted to himself, and she had the straight of it.

When she had finished, Hardison said, "There it is, Younger."

Younger inclined his head courteously and murmured, "A good bit of it true, too. I don't know what Kate says Yordy told her; I wasn't there. But I can correct her on what happened at Station, since I figured in it."

"You don't deny that you were there?" Kate asked.

"No. Not even if I could hide a dead horse overnight, I wouldn't," Younger said, amusement in his voice.

"And do you deny you thought you were meeting Yordy?"

"That's why I went."

"Then what did I say that wasn't true?"

"You said I recognized Danning and shot first at him. You didn't tell the whole truth, Kate. I simply beat him to the shot. He spoke and raised his gun. How could I see in the dark that well? I could see his bandaged hand lift the rifle, and I protected myself."

"That white bandage was covered," Kate said flatly.

Younger countered gently, "Could you see it?"

"I was upstairs. No, I couldn't see it. The veranda roof hid him, but I had told him about the bandage showing, and he's no fool. He covered it."

Younger only shook his head and smiled pityingly.

"Then let's pass that," Kate said impatiently. "You admit you were meeting Yordy. Wasn't it to pay him for the information he'd given you about Falls Canyon?"

"But I already knew that information," Younger protested good-humoredly. "If I'd wanted to hurt the Harms women that way, I could have done it a week ago. I had even," Younger said slowly, "refused to buy that information from Yordy two weeks ago when he made it to me. At Rainbow."

"Can you prove that?" Kate asked.

"If you can find me Yordy, I can."

Kate was stalemated, as Younger knew she would be. But she was stubborn too, and now she came back to her point. "Then why were you meeting Yordy? Secretly. At night. At Station, instead of town here."

"His choice, Kate, his choice," Younger said reasonably. "He was mortally afraid of Danning. If you want to know my business with him, I can tell you that, too—although it's none of your business or anybody else's." He looked at Hardison and Truscott, resentment in his hooded eyes. "Sulinam mines are building a new stamp mill in Case Valley below the mines up at Petrie, and they're letting contracts for freighting ore down to it. I bid on it. The bid is let today, as a matter of fact. If Yordy could persuade his friend Joe Briggs to sell me a couple of hundred horses for a reasonable figure, I intended to give Yordy a freighter's job. . . . You know all about the contract, John. . . . Does that satisfy you, Kate?"

He leaned back in his chair, watching Kate. She shook her head in negation and said, "No, it doesn't. If Yordy had that fine a job promised him, why did he tell us what he did about you?"

Younger leaned forward and pointed his cigar straight at Kate. "I don't know that, Kate, but I'll guess. He told it because you and Danning, by your own account, convinced him I was out to frame him. He was scared, and mad."

That was the clincher and Younger wanted to end it

here. He asked of Truscott and Hardison now, "By the way, am I on trial here?"

"Your reputation only," Walt answered quietly, and he looked at Truscott. "There's Kate's story and Younger's, John. Take your choice."

Truscott pursed his lips and looked thoughtfully at the ceiling. "I'm calling nobody a liar," he said, and looked at everyone in the room. "I go by a man's past actions. Younger's suit me."

Walt's face didn't change. "What about you, Sam?"

"I think Miles is lying," O'Hea said quietly, promptly.

There was a long, stunned silence. Younger didn't move, but a cold fear touched him.

Walt said, "Any reason?"

"The best," O'Hea said. "I heard him tell the whole story last night. Kate's version is straight."

Younger carefully put down his cigar. They were all watching him, he knew, but he had no intention of betraying the rage he felt. He came deliberately to his feet and said mildly to O'Hea, "You're sicker than I thought, or a bigger liar."

He picked up his hat from the table and strode for the door. Mac rose, and started after him when O'Hea's voice stopped him.

"Mac, move out of my office. You're through."

Mac nodded almost indifferently, and went out.

Kate and Walt looked at Truscott now. "Well, John?" Walt said.

Truscott rose from his chair, his black hat in his

hand. He shook his head, looking at his hat and said bitterly, "I've loaned him money and I'm tied up with him personally in a dozen deals. My job is to make money, and he made it. I guess you know how I've got to stand."

"Just so you know," Walt said gently.

"All right. I know," Truscott said. He nodded unhappily to them and went out.

Kate, then, did what she had been wanting to do for several minutes. She went over and kissed O'Hea on the cheek. He didn't say anything and she didn't, but he knew what the kiss was for. He looked over at Walt, who nodded and said, "Welcome home."

"It's funny," O'Hea murmured. "It feels pretty good to get off my knees." He glanced up at Kate. "Been in the kitchen this morning?"

"Not since breakfast."

"Abbie's there. If she isn't now, she will be later."

Kate smiled her slow smile and turned and went out, and when she was gone, Hardison and O'Hea were silent for several minutes, each busy with his own thoughts.

Presently, Walt stirred and said, "You're in for some trouble, Sam. How you going to meet it?"

"I don't know," O'Hea said honestly.

Chapter XV

Chris had almost reached the livery stable on his way in from Box H when he saw Miles and MacElvey leave the hotel and cross the street to Melaven's corner. He reined up, watching, and he saw Ernie Coombs step out of Melaven's corner entrance, and the three of them conferred a moment. Bill Arnold and the stumpy-legged Rainbow puncher, whose name Chris never knew, drifted to the corner too, and Chris, reading the signs, thought, *He's smart enough to be scared.*

He waited until Miles and MacElvey broke away and went up the street in the direction of the sheriff's office, and then he put up his horses and moved out and stood in the big doorway a moment. There was the problem now that he hadn't anticipated, of having to get at Miles through three or four men. He wasn't really concerned at the moment, since there were things to do first. A way was always there when the time came.

As he turned into the hotel—a tall, easy-moving man not in a hurry—he speculated on what was shaping up for Miles after the story of last night's happenings was made public. A drummer sat boredly in the first lobby chair, his feet on the sill of the window, his back to a pair of punchers talking behind him, morosely watching the small traffic of this small town.

He looked at Chris' bandaged hand without interest, and Chris, not seeing Kate behind the desk, started back for the kitchen. He was well into the dining room when the kitchen door opened and she came out. There was an expression of happiness on her face which heightened, Chris noticed, as she saw him.

He touched his hat and as she came up to him, she said, "It worked, Chris. O'Hea has deserted Miles."

Interest came into Chris' face. Kate, telling him of the meeting, sank into a chair at the nearest table and Chris, listening intently, took off his hat and sat down too.

As Kate told of O'Hea quietly puncturing Miles' story, a faint and fleeting smile crossed Chris' face and he felt a wicked pleasure. It had worked, but it was too late now. He had his chore to do.

He came to his feet and said now, "Will you take a message for Mrs. Harms? That Leach will be in for her this noon?"

Kate had started to rise, and now she sank back in her chair again. "She's going back for good? Now?"

"Della's quit," Chris said, without any censure in his statement. "Falls Canyon was fired last night, and the bunch of two-year-olds was wiped out. Della's through fighting."

"Was it Younger?"

"Yordy, I think."

Kate was silent a long time, looking at him. "What do you do now?"

"I'm through there," Chris said.

"But you can't leave Della now!" Kate said, passionately.

189

"She asked me to."

Kate's glance fell away. She rose now and walked slowly toward the lobby door, and Chris, beside her, saw the disappointment in her face. She glanced obliquely up at him and said, now, "You're going off without doing it, are you? Without wrecking Miles, or killing him?"

Her words shocked Chris to a halt, and he asked warily, "When did I say that?"

"You've never had to put it into words. To me, anyway. That's all you've wanted to do since you came here. There's nothing else you've thought about."

Chris didn't answer; his bafflement held him silent.

Kate inclined her head toward the street. "He's here today, with half his crew around him. It's a bad time, but I don't think that will stop you."

Still Chris was silent, taking the measure of her knowledge while a slow caution and alarm grew in him. It was as if he had told her what was in his heart and mind, and he had no weapon of concealment.

"You hate him almost too much to kill him, don't you? Well, there's a way to hurt him now, and badly. But you're too stubborn to see it, so go kill him."

A sudden anger touched him now as he turned and walked toward the lobby door. He was even with it when he slowed and then halted, thinking, *Damn your pride! Ask her.*

He turned and came back to her. "What way?" he asked.

Kate said unsmiling, "Sam O'Hea's upstairs. He'll

have to come down sometime, and he'll have to go to his office sometime. They're waiting for him—four or five or six of them. They'll be waiting for him from now on, every day, and he's a sick man. Go help him."

Chris frowned, eyes intent.

"He's allowed money for a deputy. Go help him. You're the only one who can."

She went back into the kitchen, then, and Chris presently turned and tramped out into the lobby. He halted once, and then walked to the street door and halted again, and presently he roused himself and walked over to the nearest chair and sat down. The drummer watched him, curious now.

Pulling out his sack of tobacco, he tried to roll a smoke with his good hand, but his mind wasn't on it, and he failed. He took out another paper and when the tobacco was in it, his fingers stilled and he stared at the paper, thinking, *I could crowd him every minute until I broke him.*

He was aware presently of someone standing in front of him and he looked up to see the drummer extending a cigar to him.

"You bother me," the drummer said morosely. "Light this up so I can quit watching you try to make that cigarette. Compliments of Beeman's Wholesale Hardware."

Chris took the cigar and the drummer went back to his chair, his face still morose.

Chris was moodily studying the street, his cigar dead in his fingers, when he heard the footsteps cease beside him and he looked up.

It was O'Hea, who said, "Hello, son. Hardison got ahold of you already?"

"Hardison? No."

"He wants to see you, to send you to me," O'Hea went on. "But hell, I don't think you're the kind that can be talked into anything, so I might as well ask you myself. Are you set on staying at Box H?"

"I'm through there," Chris said.

"Then you better see Hardison," O'Hea said. "He'll tell you about some changes around here before he sends you to me."

"I heard about the changes," Chris said slowly.

O'Hea looked squarely at him. "All right. I need a deputy, and I want you. Will you think it over?"

"I have. I'll work for you."

"When?"

"Now."

O'Hea's slow, unaccustomed smile came, and Chris rose. Together in silence, they went out and Chris adjusted his pace to O'Hea's careful walk toward his office.

In the middle of the block, O'Hea said, "Just one thing. Miles is waiting for me at the office."

"I figured that," Chris said.

O'Hea looked obliquely at him and said nothing. They went on downstreet and waited for a freight wagon to pull past into the lumber yard, and then went into the sheriff's office.

Out of the habit, O'Hea tramped past the first door

and entered the anteroom. Ernie Coombs, young Bill Arnold and Stew Shallis were seated in the anteroom. Ernie's chair was by the office door, back-tilted against the wall, and his heels were hooked over the bottom rung of it.

Ernie was already grinning derisively at O'Hea before he caught sight of Chris, and his grin still held as he said, "Go on in, Pop. You're goin' to get your head unscrewed."

He brought his chair down on all four legs as O'Hea passed him and went into the office. He started to rise and Chris put out his hand and gently shoved him back into the chair.

"This is a waiting room. You wait."

He paused long enough to see Ernie's mouth open a little in surprise, and Ernie looked at the other two Rainbow hands. They didn't move.

Chris stepped into the office and closed the door behind him.

Younger Miles was standing in the middle of the room. His glance, hot and bold, settled on Chris, and Chris put his back against the wall next the chair where MacElvey sat. Chris could tell Younger's anger over last night was mixed with his anger over O'Hea's desertion.

Younger said roughly to O'Hea, "Get that drifter out of here."

"Meet my deputy," O'Hea replied, with a quiet irony.

Younger looked long at O'Hea and then said gently, "So that's it?"

"That, and more," O'Hea said quietly. "Abbie started work in her old job this morning. You annoy her just once, Younger, and I'll load up a shotgun with rusty nails and shoot you in the belly." He paused a moment to let that sink in, then said, "Anything you have to say to me in an official way, you can say to Danning. I wrote my letter, you see, and I'm back on duty." He smiled. "Now say it, and then get out."

Miles' bull neck colored a deep red, but his face was composed, almost pleasant. "It'll keep," he murmured, "until he's out of office."

He looked once more at Chris, his eyes still hot and full of rage. "You brace me just once, drifter, and you're dead."

He strode toward the corridor door and yanked it open and went out. Mac rose and quietly followed him, and then Chris pushed away from the wall and opened the door into the anteroom. Ernie and Bill Arnold and Shallis were standing in the center of the room, regarding the door.

"Go on," Chris murmured. "Didn't you hear him whistle?"

The three of them headed slowly for the door. Chris stepped back in the office just in time to see O'Hea gather a pile of papers and an aged yellow slicker from the table and tramp over to the open corridor door.

When Bill Arnold, last out, was just passing in the corridor, O'Hea shoved the stuff at him and said, "These are Mac's. Give 'em to him."

194

Arnold grabbed for the bundle, his face sullen, and a scattering of papers drifted off the bottom of the pile and spilled on the floor.

Bill hesitated and O'Hea said, "Get out!" and Bill went.

O'Hea started to bend to pick up the papers on the floor, and then grunted and stood erect, holding his side. Chris went out into the hall and picked up the papers and came back in with them. Looking at them, he saw they were fresh sheets of stationery with the printed letterhead, "Sulinam Mines, Inc."

Both sides were blank, and he went over to the wastebasket and dumped them in. When he looked at O'Hea, the old man winked solemnly.

"Well, let's get you sworn in, son."

Younger and MacElvey paused at Melaven's corner and waited for Ernie, Arnold and Shallis. Younger's face, Mac noticed, held the same expression as Ernie Coombs' when they all gathered on the corner. It was an expression of edgy, wild temper, as if the wrong inflection on a word might set off the explosion.

Ernie's greeting was indicative. He looked levelly at Younger, his bleak eyes wicked. "You goin' to take that?"

Younger didn't even bother to answer him. "You and Bill and Stew go up to Tip's shack and hold it. Move a big crew up tomorrow and finish it in a hurry. If Danning tries to stop you, that's all we want."

Ernie grinned faintly before he and Shallis moved

off downstreet for their horses. Bill hesitated long enough to dump the papers O'Hea had given him in Mac's arms, and then followed them. Younger watched them moodily for a moment, and then his baleful glance shifted to the hotel. "She's going to get out of there, Mac," he said grimly.

"You better stay away from her this noon," Mac said quietly.

The glance Younger gave him was brief and wrathful. "I'm not eating any place where my wife is kitchen help."

A puncher passed and spoke to him, and Younger didn't even hear him. He was again looking at the hotel, and now he seemed to have made up his mind.

He nodded toward Melaven's and said, "I'll be in here." He looked full at Mac now, without anger. "The Petrie stage will be in at two. Bring the mail over."

Mac nodded and Younger went on into the saloon. Mac went up street with his gear and turned into the store. Younger's reference to the Petrie stage, he knew, meant that this afternoon they would know if they had low bid on the Sulinam job. Mac stored his papers away in the bottom drawer of his desk, which he locked, and then went across to the hotel.

He was one of the last of the diners and he ate a leisurely meal by himself. When the last customer had left the dining room, he finished quickly and rose, but instead of going out into the lobby, he headed for the kitchen. There he spoke to the big, cheerful-seeming woman who was cook, and to the waitresses who were cleaning up the dishes, and then he poked his head in the door of the big room which was the pantry.

Abbie Miles was already laying out pans for the supper pies. She wore a full apron over her dress and her sleeves were rolled elbow-high. She heard Mac and turned, and when she saw him, she smiled. Mac noted with no surprise that the sullenness and defiance that had always been in her face was gone; she seemed cheerful and happy as she said to him now, "Hello, Mac. Are you the ambassador?"

Mac leaned against a counter and shook his head. "No, I just came to see how you were."

"How do I look?"

"Beautiful," Mac said simply.

Abbie flushed, and looked down at the pans. She said, without looking at him, "Please don't say that again, Mac. It doesn't get us anywhere. I'm still a married woman."

"I know. I only answered your question."

Abbie half smiled at him, and then her expression sobered. "What has he said about my leaving?"

"He says you're coming back."

A look of faint alarm came into Abbie's face. "But I'm not. What can I do if he insists?"

"Your Dad had a pretty good idea. Load up a shotgun with rusty nails and shoot him."

Abbie's hand stopped moving. "Did you say a 'good' idea, Mac? That's the first time I've heard you say anything against Younger."

"My tongue slipped," Mac said dryly.

"If you feel that way, why do you work for him?" Abbie said slowly. "Did you take an oath to cherish him until death do you part, like I did? You can quit. Why don't you?"

"Money. Food. It's a living. It's exciting. I'm crazy. Take your choice, only let's not talk about it," Mac said, wryly, and he smiled his faint, twisted smile.

"There seem to be a lot of things neither of us can talk about," Abbie said softly.

"And I'll add one more to the list," Mac said with quiet firmness. "We won't talk about liquor any more, Abbie. I've lived with that on my conscience long enough. If you've got to have it, get it from someone else. I've loved you enough so I'd do anything you ask, anything. But not that any more."

"But I don't want it," Abbie said proudly. "I don't ever want to see any again. I don't know why that's over with, but it is."

Mac smiled and nodded once. "I know why. So do you."

"All right, I do."

"Keep it over with. Pretty soon, even the reason you once had will be gone."

Abbie regarded him a long moment. "My marriage to Younger? Why do you say that?"

Mac straightened up and smiled faintly. "A hunch. Good-by, my dear."

"Good-by, Mac," Abbie said slowly, and she watched him go out, a puzzlement reflected in her face.

Passing through the lobby, Mac glanced at the clock and saw it was past stage time. He crossed to Melaven's, sought the other corner and walked on to Waycross' hardware store, a front corner of which, walled away by racks and pigeon-holes, was Triumph's post office. Stepping in line behind two other townsmen, he moved up to the wicket and when his turn came said to Waycross behind it, "Hello, Ed. What's for us?"

He was handed a string-tied bundle of mail, and he went over to the counter and looked through its contents. When he came to a long slim envelope bearing the printed legend in the upper left hand corner, SULINAM MINES, INC., he took it out and put it in his coat pocket, gathered up the mail and went out.

His pace back to the store was unhurried. Walking down the main aisle, he saw through the open door that Younger was standing in front of the big window by his desk, hands in hip pockets. Younger turned restlessly, saw MacElvey and strode swiftly to the door, where they met.

"What?" Younger said.

Mac said nothing, only handed him the envelope from his coat pocket. Younger tore open the envelope and in his haste to remove the letter, dropped both. He swore softly, and picked up the letter, opened and read it. An odd expression, Mac noticed—one of both anger and pleasure—came into his broad face as he finished it. He looked up, extending the letter to Mac, saying, "We got it."

Mac, standing, read the letter written in a clerk's legible script under the letterhead of SULINAM MINES, INC.

Dear Mr. Miles: We take satisfaction in informing you that your offer to move a minimum of 175,000 tons of ore from our mines in Petrie to the stamp mill in Case Valley at a cost to this corporation of $3.16 per ton, was the lowest offer received by us, and accordingly we are ready to sign the contract.

Mr. Amos Hardy, with whom Mr. MacElvey of your firm discussed details of specifications and who is treasurer of Sulinam Mines, Inc., left for the East yesterday to return in ten days' time. Since he is required to countersign all contracts of this nature, may I suggest that he and I meet with you in Triumph immediately upon his return, the 25th of the present month.

May we respectfully call your attention to paragraph 14 of the published specifications, a copy of which Mr. MacElvey requested from us, which states that a minimum of five hundred tons of ore is to be put down at the Case Valley stamp mill not later than November 30, 1879.

We anticipate the most cordial relations between yourself and Sulinam Mines, Inc., and look forward to a long and mutually prosperous association.

Respectfully yours,

Ivan H. Coe, *General Mgr.*

Sulinam Mines, Inc.

Mac smiled faintly and folded the letter and looked at Younger. He had gone back to the window, and was staring through it at the distant Blackbows bulking to the south.

He turned now and said grimly, "A hell of a time for it to come."

"You haven't signed the contract yet," Mac said softly.

"Are you suggesting I don't?"

"You're the one that's worried, not me."

Younger swung around and looked out the window again. "I'm not worried. If I get that drifter, O'Hea'll pull in his horns. And I won't quit till I get him."

He came over to Mac and took the letter and read it again. Then he sighed heavily, as a man does who is starting in on a long and heavy task. "All right, get it going, Mac. Coe is watching that deadline as close as we are. What's the name of your surveyor—Travis? Start him over to Petrie right away. Get your telegram written to Dan and tell him to close for the horses and start 'em up here. Get the one off for the wagons, too, and tell Sholtz to pay cash, of course. I'll ride over to the tie camp tonight and see that Brush sobers up the road crew and gets 'em moving. We can start a wagon off from here tonight with the tools and grub enough to get the first two road camps going. Draw on the store for everything you need. Talbot is going to have to put a lot of feed down there for the road teams, so I'll put the crew on the barns first. Write your telegrams so I can take them with me, and I'll send a man from here to Moorehouse. You—" he gestured impatiently. "Hell, you know all this, Mac, just get it going."

Mac nodded, no excitement in his face, and picked up the letter and read it again. Younger regarded him thoughtfully.

"Mac, either I'm going to be rich enough after this, so I won't have to worry about money again, or so broke I won't have any to worry about."

"You're spending the biggest chunk of your money now before the contract is signed, you know," Mac murmured.

Miles gestured briefly, angrily to the letter. "If I wait for Hardy, I lose ten days. And those ten days will make the difference between meeting the deadline and forfeiting. What's the matter with that letter? It's good in any court. Why question it?"

"I'm a careful man," Mac said.

"So am I, up to a point, and that point's past," Younger said, smiling faintly. "Come on, Mac. Get going."

Chapter XVI

Mrs. Harms was pretty well posted on events by Leach when she reached home in the early afternoon. She and Della cried a bit in each other's arms when they met, while Leach carried in Mrs. Harms' trunk. Andy rode in a little later and turned his horse out, but did not come to the house. He'd been up to Falls

Canyon to have his look and to check if the fire was out, or had spread.

Mrs. Harms ate something, and presently sent Leach to get Andy, and Leach found him sitting atop the corral fence moodily chewing a straw and regarding the distant flats. There was a faint cloudiness between them and the sun now.

"Mrs. Harms wants you and me at the house," Leach told him, and Andy climbed down. He didn't speak to Leach, and Leach didn't speak to him.

When Andy saw Mrs. Harms in the lean-to, he took off his hat and shook hands with her and told her he was glad she was back, which he was. Della was seated at the big table and Mrs. Harms sat down at the head of it. Andy sat at his accustomed place and Leach took the chair beside him. This, Andy knew, was to be a discussion of Box H affairs, since it had often happened in the past.

Mrs. Harms began by looking at Andy and saying, "Della tells me you think Leach is to blame for what happened last night, Andy. Well, I don't think so and Della doesn't, so we won't talk about it any more."

"I don't have to talk about it any more," Andy said. "I know what I know."

"Now, that's enough," Mrs. Harms said placidly. "We have enough trouble without you boys jawing. We have a lot of money to pay back, and we've got to figure what's best to do."

All of them nodded and Mrs. Harms said, almost absently, "I suppose Mr. Danning wasn't all trouble.

He got us back Thessaly."

Leach said, "He said something this mornin' that surprised me. Tip Henry's lit out." He looked at Mrs. Harms. "Don't that make his homestead void, Mrs. Harms?"

"Why, yes," Mrs. Harms said. "You have to live on the land you homestead at least six months out of the year until you prove up. Otherwise, a rich man like Younger Miles could buy all the government land he wanted to."

"Then what happens to Tip's homestead?" Leach asked.

"At the end of the year when he hasn't proven up, it's public domain again, isn't it?" Della said.

"But if anybody moves in there, he's trespassin', ain't he?" Leach asked.

Mrs. Harms said, "Of course. Why?"

"Andy said Danning said there wasn't anybody there the other day. Why don't we move in on it, then? We'd be trespassin', but Tip Henry won't be there to complain. Younger Miles can't complain, because he's got nothin' to do with it. Besides, Thessaly's ours, and that shack is in Thessaly."

"Who'd you say moves in?" Andy cut in.

"We do," Leach said.

"Who's we?"

"Why, me or you," Leach said. "We finish the shack and use it like we do the Salt Meadow line shack."

"And Miles lets you," Andy said, with something very like irony in his voice. He looked at the two

204

women. "You know why Tip Henry jumped the country? He was scared of Danning—plumb scared to death. You got anybody workin' for you now, Mrs. Harms, that's goin' to scare anybody?"

"Nonsense," Mrs. Harms, said tartly. "Grown men like Tip Henry don't scare. He was probably good and sick of Younger Miles and Ernie Coombs, and wanted to stay out of trouble."

Andy said nothing. He liked the easy common-sense way Mrs. Harms usually talked, but this wasn't common sense.

Della was watching Leach, frowning. "Isn't that breaking the law, Leach?"

Leach said, "We ain't hurtin' Tip Henry, are we? He don't care. We're only beatin' Miles to it."

"Then why don't we do it?" Della asked suddenly, and looked at Andy. "You were talking pretty big a couple of days ago, Andy, wanting us to stand up for our rights. What about it?"

"What right we got there?" Andy asked.

"What right have we to Thessaly?" Mrs. Harms put in. "None, except it's always belonged to us. Tip's quarter section will revert to the same thing Thessaly is in another year. Why shouldn't we move in and keep Miles out?"

Andy couldn't deny the facts, which sounded reasonable enough, but he had a feeling this wasn't the whole story. He knew there were more than rights involved. Fear of Danning had stopped the building of that shack. On the other hand, Box H had to fight.

Danning had as good as said it when he asked him to stay. If Box H suddenly turned timid now, Rainbow would walk all over them. Andy had learned that much since Danning had been with them. And nobody could deny that Box H had more right than Rainbow to claim the quarter section Tip Henry had given up.

Andy said slowly, "Well, I'm workin' for you and your mother, Della, but we got two men against Rainbow's fifteen, if it comes to a fight."

Nobody thought that deserved comment, and the talk turned to the consequences of last night's fire. It was agreed that they must recall all feed contracts and ask for an extension on the note. Andy was only half-listening; his slow, methodical mind was still considering the move to the shack in Thessaly, and he was silent until Mrs. Harms rose, saying, "If you're going up to the shack, I'd better get some food ready for you."

"Is that an order, Mrs. Harms?" Andy asked reluctantly.

"Yes. We have to look sharp now, Andy," Mrs. Harms answered, her tone neither brusque nor kindly, but matter-of-fact.

"It looks like it's clouding over," Andy said lamely.

Della stood up and said, "What I said this morning still goes, Andy. When you don't like it, all you got to do is to see Truscott."

Andy didn't reply, because there was nothing more really to say. But Leach, hiding behind the skirts of these women, unable or unwilling to accept any responsibility, but eager enough to butter them up, was to blame. Della said she would ride up to have a look at Falls Canyon, and asked Andy to saddle her horse.

He went out, and Leach fell in beside him.

"Scared of Miles?" Leach demanded slyly, when they were away from the house.

"Him and ten or fifteen others put together, I am."

"But we got a right there."

"Tell him that."

"I aim to, if he comes up."

"If he comes up, you'll be there," Andy said grimly.

They saddled three horses and packed a fourth horse with saws, axes and ropes. Andy led the horses out of the corral and stepped into the saddle. Leach led the fourth horse over to the cottonwood where Della, dressed in riding clothes now, was waiting. Andy noticed she was pale and worried, but he knew it wasn't about what they were going to do. She was worried about losing Danning, knowing the prop had been knocked from under Box H.

They rode across the flats abreast, and took the trail to the bench and were presently at the forks where the trail to Thessaly left the trail to Falls.

Leach reined up then and said to Andy, "You go on ahead and I'll cut across from Falls. I'm goin' with Della."

"You're comin' with me," Andy said flatly, his homely face stubborn.

Leach bristled. "I'm goin' up and cut out a

hindquarter of beef from one of them carcasses and bring it over to Thessaly. I don't care if you eat it or not, but I aim to. What are you goin' to do about that?"

"He's going over to Thessaly, Leach. Now stop wrangling, you two," Della said.

Leach set off on the Salt Meadow trail without another word and Andy took the Thessaly trail. In the back of his mind was the thought that this was going to be a test for Leach, and one he wouldn't be allowed to dodge. Leach had thought this up, and Leach was going to see it through.

Andy climbed steadily through the timber. At each open park there was Rainbow beef grazing, and the sight of them reminded Andy that he was in unfriendly country. He thought of his last ride through here in the night with Danning, and he squirmed a little when he recalled his innocence on that morning. But wasn't he doing the same thing now, only, instead of being innocent, he was being badgered into it by people who didn't understand.

When he came to where he and Danning had boiled coffee that morning, he saw the holed coffeepot lying on its side in the grass by the trail. There was something vaguely sinister in the fact that it should still be there where he could see it, warning him.

But when he rode into the clearing where the shack was, it was deserted. It was just as he and Danning had left it, with the logs scattered helter-skelter, the chuck wagon gone, the walls still two-thirds raised, and even the turf still holding the heel gouges of the fight. This was somehow reassuring to Andy as he dismounted. Perhaps Rainbow had given up the idea of finishing the shack, now that Tip had been chased off and Box H cattle moved into the canyon.

He took the pack off the second horse, put hobbles on him and his own horse, and turned them out across the stream. He could see a few Box H cattle grazing up the canyon, and this was reassuring, too. When he had finished making camp, there were still some hours of fast-clouding daylight left. It would rain tonight, Andy thought gloomily. Leach would be along presently, and Andy decided to put in some work while he waited.

Accordingly, he set about notching the logs that were scattered about, swinging the big double-bitted ax with an easy strength. He had worked only a few minutes when he discovered that the six-gun rammed in the waistband of his jeans got in his way. Taking it out, he laid it on a log, and immediately decided it wouldn't be of much use to him there if he had to use it in a hurry. Thinking it over a moment, he compromised. He went over to his pack and brought out his rifle, which he tilted against a nearby log. Mentally, he resolved to always be working close to one or the other, and then he set about his work again.

As he worked now, he became absorbed in it, taking a solid, nameless pleasure in watching the ax bite deeply and accurately into the logs and sending big heavy chips flying as if impelled from a gun. He moved from one log to another, notching only one end now before measuring, and the big muscles of his shoulders began to loosen, and he sweat. There was nothing in his mind except a deep contentment.

He was swinging long, crisp downstrokes on one of the few dry logs when the feeling came to him that he was being watched. It came suddenly, inexplicably, and he looked up.

There was Ernie Coombs standing some ten feet away regarding him with those cold and humorless bleak eyes. Stew Shallis stood beside him. Andy wiped his forehead with his sleeve, pushed his hat back on his head, and used that moment to turn his head so he could glance at his rifle.

Bill Arnold was standing where the rifle had stood, and he had it in his hand. Andy knew his six-gun was behind him and he wondered if someone had that, too, but he didn't turn. He was caught cold. He dropped his arm slowly and Ernie Coombs said, "Finishin' it for Henhouse?"

There was something baleful and ugly in Ernie's tone, as if all he wanted was proof.

Andy sized up the three men carefully, and he felt a cold fear touch him inside. He'd been caught red-handed in something that was really important to them.

Slowly, he tried to marshal the facts in his favor that Leach and Della had spoken this morning, and now he had less faith in them than he had had then.

"It's Tip Henry's place, and he's run out," Andy said.

"And he told you to take over," Bill Arnold jibed angrily.

"He never told anybody to take over," Andy said doggedly. "First one here gets it."

Ernie said quietly, ominously, "I watched you scare Tip off and take over the canyon. And now you steal a half-built shack we threw up and figure to move us off. Try it, startin' now."

He moved toward Andy, reaching with his left hand for the gun in its holster at his side. Andy knew dismally this was it, and he also knew he was going down fighting. He wheeled and ran for the log behind him on which he had laid his six-gun.

It wasn't there. They'd got that, too.

In the fleeting part of a second, Andy understood he had been crowded into going for a gun that wasn't there, so that they were blameless.

He heard the first shot and tried to stop running; he was giving up. The second shot he didn't hear. Something hit him and all sound, all sight, all will, all thought ribboned off thinly and stopped, and he came to rest with his face in the grass.

Chapter XVII

Kate took a last look around the kitchen, saw everything was in order and blew out the lamp. Moving into the dining room, she walked over to blow out the lamp, above the long center table, and in passing she shoved two chairs back into place. The act of doing so reminded her of something and she paused, looking again at the two chairs. Yes, this was where she and Chris had sat this morning when they talked.

She blew out the lamp, wondering now what had prompted her to do what she'd done this morning. There was little enough self-deception in her that she knew she had wanted Chris Danning to stay here. She acted like any woman afraid of losing her man, and he angered and baffled her.

Fred Musgrove and Abe Wildman, from Ed Lavendar's outfit, were yawning in the lobby chairs, and Kate spoke to them and went upstairs, through the dark parlor, and out onto the veranda roof.

Walt was in his chair, and Kate pulled another beside him, saying, "I thought Abbie and her father were with you."

"They quit me for a cribbage game," Walt said quietly, and then he added, "Funny what self-respect will do for a man, Sam looks better already."

"You couldn't see him," Kate said.

"I could feel it. It's in his voice and what he talks about, and the way he talks to Abbie."

Kate didn't answer. She was staring quietly at the half-dark street. Presently, Walt said, "It'll rain soon. I can smell it."

Kate didn't answer, and Walt was silent too. The minutes passed, and Kate stirred restlessly and was quiet again. Suddenly she said, "Why didn't he thank me, Walt? Or even tell me?"

"He doesn't like to be beholden to anybody, I reckon." Walt looked at her. "This is Danning we're talking about, isn't it? You didn't mention any name."

Kate laughed softly at herself, and Walt said, "What put it into your head to send him to Sam?"

"I didn't want to see him go," Kate said honestly. "Don't ask me why, because I don't know. A week ago I wanted him chased out of town."

"You want to get even with Miles for the way he's treated Abbie, maybe."

"Yes, but that wasn't it."

"Then you like him."

"Yes," Kate agreed, looking at him. "I do. Why?"

"He's a surly devil," Walt observed.

"And rude and insolent and untactful and thankless, yet I like him."

"You feel sorry for him. It's him against Miles."

"Feel sorry for him?" Kate echoed. "Sorry like I do for a grizzly bear. He'll kill Miles. I'm sure of that."

"Ah," Walt said. "If you've seen that, then quit liking him, Katie. As long as a man's got a grudge, he's no good. He'll trample people, and he's too selfish to know he's doing it. He'll hurt you."

"But you like him. You said so," Kate countered.

Walt said gently, "I'm not a girl. It doesn't hurt me when he doesn't thank me when he should. Or when he doesn't tell me his business. Or when what I say goes against what he thinks, and he says so."

Kate had no answer for that, but she thought about it. It was as close as Walt ever came to advising her, and he was dead serious about it, and she supposed he was right.

"If they don't tame by themselves, Katie, you can't tame 'em. And now I'd like a pipe, please."

Kate sat still a rebellious and chastened moment, and then rose. She looked down into the street as she turned, and something down there caught her attention and held it. It was a small man on the ridden horse leading another horse, and over the back of the second horse was a canvas-wrapped bundle. A pair of boots hung below the canvas, and the general shape of the bulk was unmistakable.

She leaned forward and looked closely, and when she was sure it was Leach Conover she called, "Who is it, Leach?"

Leach looked up. "Andy West," he said, and he turned the corner and went up the street to the sheriff's office.

After supper Chris got a solitary drink at Melaven's and watched the faro game for an hour, and afterward went back to the sheriff's office. Lighting the lamp, he took off his hat and threw it in one of the chairs and sank slowly into O'Hea's chair. He was going to have to see Kate tonight and acknowledge his debt to her for this new job, but he was putting it off. The way she read him today, heart, soul and mind, still troubled him.

Painstakingly, he rolled a cigarette and lighted it, watched the blue smoke hanging motionless in the still lamplit air, and a strange discouragement was on him. He knew why. This morning, he had thought this would end today, and it had not, and he was no nearer the end. He had even got a room over the barbershop this afternoon; he was here for a while. He wondered, almost furtively, what he would do after he had killed Miles, and he did not know. He had never thought beyond that point because he had never wanted to, and yet tonight he wondered for idle minutes.

Purposely, then, with a feeling of guilt, he thought of Bess, reaching back in his mind for the place in his fantasy where he had left her. But it was no good tonight either. Memory, he reflected bitterly, was a fragile thing, perishable as all things are perishable, and he hated it.

He heard footsteps in the corridor, and presently the anteroom door was opened and Leach Conover stepped in. Leach's clean wash-faded levis and shirt had spots of blood on them. His bitter eyes held a quick surprise as he saw Chris in O'Hea's chair, and he said sourly, "Where's O'Hea?"

"Sleeping, likely. What do you want of him?"

"Why should I tell you?" Leach demanded truculently.

"I'm his deputy."

Leach thought about this a long moment, then shrugged. "Andy's shot. I got him outside on his horse, dead."

Chris felt a sickening wrench deep within him, and he sat there motionless, looking at Leach, understanding this only with difficulty. Leach, however, started in with the dreary story of Box H's decision to occupy Tip's homestead, of his parting from Andy, and of his own approach to Thessaly. He had heard the shots, dismounted, crawled through the timber, and seen Stew Shallis, Ernie Coombs and Bill Arnold standing over Andy. They had put down Andy's rifle and six-gun, which they, strangely, had possession of, on separate logs and departed. Andy had been shot in the back. O'Hea, roused by Kate, came in during Leach's story, and silently took a chair and listened.

When Leach finished, Chris' gray eyes were cold with hatred.

He said then, "Did you have a gun on you, Leach?"

Leach eyed him warily. "I did, but I wasn't takin' on any three men."

"No," Chris said, and all his contempt for Leach was in that one word. There was something else he wanted answered, and he voiced it now. "Whose idea was it to move into Tip's place?"

Leach regarded him carefully. "All of us. We had more right there than Rainbow, now that Tip was gone."

"Who gave the order?"

"Mrs. Harms."

"How'd she know Tip was gone?"

"I told her. You told us this morning."

"So it was your idea?" Chris murmured.

"You said they were gone. How'd I know they'd come back?"

A feeling of gray hopelessness touched Chris then, and he looked at O'Hea. "Have we got a jail?"

"Yes. Back end." O'Hea was puzzled.

Chris rose. "Show me."

O'Hea stood up and walked past Leach into the anteroom. Chris motioned Leach to go ahead, but Leach was suspicious. "Where we goin'?"

"You're going to be locked up where you can't hurt anybody else," Chris said, walking toward him.

Leach made a grab for the gun in his belt and Chris simply leaned against his slight body, pinning him to the door. He put his left hand swiftly over the hammer of Leach's half-drawn gun and twisted the gun out of Leach's hand. It was done quickly, contemptuously, easily.

O'Hea had stopped in the anteroom. Now Chris shoved Leach at him and said mildly, "Lead the way, O'Hea."

Leach snarled over his shoulder, "You can't do it, you damn drifter! I'll have Mrs. Harms get a lawyer that'll run you out of the country!"

Chris didn't answer. Each time Leach would stop in the corridor to curse him, Chris would shove him gently along. O'Hea lighted a lamp down the corridor and then opened the door at the end of the corridor and lighted the lamp in the big room beyond. The jail itself was a large room, running the width of the building, with three barred windows close to its high ceiling. A third of the length of the room there were bars running from the floor to a heavy ceiling beam, and there was a barred door in the middle which stood open. It reflected a crude but effective blacksmithing job. There was only the one big cell, which held four cots along the wall.

Chris, with O'Hea watching, shoved Leach into the cell and locked the door with the key O'Hea extended. Leach was still cursing shrilly as Chris and O'Hea stepped out into the corridor.

Chris tramped back into the office and picked up his hat. He felt O'Hea watching him, and now O'Hea, waiting for an opportunity, said mildly, "You can't do that, Chris. What's he in there for?"

"I told him," Chris said grimly. "He's got a man killed, and he lost those two women six thousand dollars, all in a couple of days. I've got to talk to Della. He can't stay on."

"But he's in jail," O'Hea pointed out.

"He was a witness to a murder, wasn't he? Can't you hold a man on that?"

O'Hea said he could, and only then did Chris realize he was still holding Leach's gun in his hand. He tossed it toward the table, where it landed and skidded off, falling to the floor underneath. He went over to the table and knelt and picked up the gun, and then he saw, within reach, the sheet of MacElvey's paper that he had neglected this afternoon. He picked it up, and as soon as he had it he saw it was a folded sheet of paper, unlike MacElvey's stuff. Unfolding it, he read in printed letters which he knew instantly had been used to disguise the handwriting: "Miles is moving in on Tip Henry's homestead." It was unsigned. Chris, behind his anger, made an effort to pull his mind back to this. Somebody close enough to Miles to know his plans had shoved the note under the door, probably when the office was locked for the supper hour. He puzzled at it a moment, knowing only one thing, that there was a traitor in Miles' crew. The information wasn't of any value now, but if Andy West hadn't been killed, it would have been. Chris folded the note and put it in his pocket while O'Hea, seated now, watched him.

Chris rifled through the gear on the table and turned up an unopened box of shotgun shells, buckshot load. He rammed a handful of them in his pocket, and then tramped over to the gun rack and took down a double-barreled shotgun. He looked at O'Hea now.

"I'm going to get Shallis and Coombs and Arnold. That all right with you?"

O'Hea nodded silently.

"Will you take care of Andy?" He nodded toward the street, and again O'Hea nodded assent. O'Hea was watching him curiously, and now he said, "That bunch will fight. They'll claim it was self-defense and that Leach is lying, and Miles will back 'em."

"Let him," Chris said, and went out.

When he hit the street he paused and looked at the canvas-wrapped burden on Andy's horse, which stood uneasily at the tie rail. *I told him to stay,* he thought somberly, and a deep sadness was in him as he remembered Andy's stout defense of him to Della. Andy was dead, but the Rainbow man who killed him would die, too, Chris thought grimly, and as he turned upstreet, he was already considering what lay ahead. He discarded immediately the notion of taking his saddle horse to Rainbow. He was going to bring back three men, and he had no intention of riding herd on them at night when they could break and scatter in three different directions. A buckboard and team would be better. He looked up at the sky, black and starless with its promise of coming rain.

At Melaven's, where a trio of punchers lounged in the doorway of the saloon, he turned the corner and was almost past the saloon when a passing rider called, "Danning?"

Chris stopped. The light from Melaven's lamps only dimly touched the shape of the man who had called. The rider pulled his horse around now and came over to the tie rail. It was the chunky Rainbow hand, Chris saw, one of the men who had been in the office with Miles that afternoon.

"Andy West was killed this afternoon up at Tip Henry's place," the rider said. "Three of us caught him workin' on Tip's shack, planning to take over. When we jumped him, he pulled a gun on us. It was us or him, and he got it."

Chris looked carefully at the man's broad, thick-lipped face, and said, "Who are you?"

"Stew Shallis."

"Get down, Shallis," Chris said, walking slowly toward the end of the tie rail and coming to a halt beside Shallis' horse.

"What for?"

"I'm arresting you."

Shallis laughed then, and he spoke loudly now, for the benefit of the loafers in Melaven's door. "I rode all the way in here to tell you what had happened and to give that crazy Andy West a chance to be buried decent. He grabbed for his gun and we beat him to it. If that ain't self-defense, I don't know what is. You ain't arresting me for protectin' myself, and you can tell O'Hea I said so."

"Get down," Chris said quietly.

"I'm ridin' out of here, now, and you ain't stopping me."

He lifted his reins. Chris tucked his shotgun under his arm and put his good hand under the stirrup of Shallis' saddle and heaved.

Shallis, taken unawares, didn't have the length of leg to hug his horse, and he slanted sideways out of the saddle, grabbing wildly at the horn.

He landed heavily in the dust and Chris stepped around the rump of his horse. Shallis rolled over, still on his side and tugged at the gun in his holster. Chris kicked his hand away from it and then reached down and buried his hand in Shallis' kinky hair and dragged him the ten feet into the light from the saloon door. Shallis forgot his gun; he put both hands on Chris' wrist to keep from having his hair pulled out. When Chris had him in the light, he toed Shallis' gun from its holster with his boot and then let go of his hair.

Shallis rolled over on his knees and swung clumsily

at Chris' belly, and Chris put a foot on his chest and shoved, and Shallis went over on his back in the dust.

The shotgun hung down from Chris' hand; he didn't even raise it as he said quietly, "You know where you're going. Get up."

Shallis cursed him, coming to his feet, and Chris didn't move. Shallis' clothes ribboned small streamers of dust into the road as he stood there, squat and spraddle-legged, his back to the men who were watching this from Melaven's door. The rage in him increased now as he saw the uselessness of fighting. He turned and said savagely to the men in the saloon doorway, "You goin' to let him do that to an innocent man?"

Chris didn't move. There was a long silence, and then someone said dryly, "Looks that way, sonny." There was a murmur of laughter after that and Shallis, cursing bitterly, circled around and picked up his hat and tramped stiff-legged past the saloon toward the sheriff's office.

The first few drops of rain fell now, Chris noticed, as he followed Shallis downstreet past the barber shop and the high fence and closed gates of the lumberyard. He turned him over to O'Hea in the office, and after that he stepped down the corridor and into the cell block, closing the door after him. Leach was sitting on the edge of his cot, still furious, and he watched Chris with a bitter and venomous dislike.

"I've got Shallis out there, Leach," Chris said. "He'll be put in with you, like Arnold and Coombs when they're caught. When they're tried for Andy's murder, you'll be the only witness against them. If they ever find out you saw it, then it will have to come from you, not from us. If they do, they'll likely kill you and I hope they do."

Leach cursed him, and Chris went out, passing O'Hea and Shallis in the corridor. He paused in the doorway, watching the slow rain pock the heavy dust of the street and wondering how it would affect his plans.

There was a loose horse, saddled, standing in the middle of the street, and Chris recognized it as Shallis'. The horse had probably followed Shallis down the street. Chris was about to step over and catch the reins when the horse, who saw him, shifted its head faintly and pricked up its ears. It was looking at something barely upstreet, and now it snorted softly.

Curious, Chris watched him, not moving. The horse took a few steps toward the boardwalk, then stopped, still looking in the same direction, and not at Chris.

Chris still held the shotgun in his hand. He stepped cautiously out into the rain and looked toward Melaven's, then glanced at the horse again. The horse was still looking straight ahead of him, in the direction of the lumberyard next door. Chris' glance shifted to the double board gates of the drive. They had been closed when he passed with Shallis; they were ajar now, and the horse, looking for Shallis, was alert to the fact there was somebody behind them.

Chris stepped back into the doorway, considering

this. Had Shallis been told off to feel out the ground by Miles, who had every intention of fighting this out if his men were arrested? Chris didn't know, but somebody was waiting behind the gate, and he was going to find out who it was.

He flattened himself against the building and moved onto the boardwalk, and then softly moved downstreet in the opposite direction from the lumberyard. When he came to the bridge over the Coroner, he turned down the alley that followed its bank until he came to the cross alley that passed by the rear of the jail and the lumberyard. The slow rain and the river's rush hushed his footfalls as he tramped back toward the lumberyard.

The fence here in the rear of the yard was high too, the gate shut. He tried to scale the fence, but one-handed he could not; and he turned away to search for something to climb on. When he found it—a sturdy crate by a woodshed across the alley—he moved it against the fence, but not before he carefully pushed his shotgun under the gate.

With the aid of the box, he climbed the wall and dropped to the ground inside the lumberyard which was utterly dark. Retrieving his gun now, he moved in against the piles of stacked lumber and silently worked his way toward the front gate. The rain made a soft plashing murmur on the new boards, which smelled cleanly of pitch.

Presently he came to the last pile of lumber. Beyond, was the lumber company office. Now he could see the dim light from the street through the four-foot gap in the gates. He listened, and presently, from a spot in the gloom against the office, he heard Ernie Coombs' voice whisper curses at Shallis' horse, and another man's voice grunted assent. They were so close it startled him.

He raised the shotgun hip high now, and said in an iron voice, "Walk this way, Ernie. I've got a shotgun on you."

There were two seconds of silence, and then a pair of shots, one on the heel of the other, blasted the night. Chris saw a movement toward the gate, and he raised his gun, and when the figure driving through the gate was framed in the light, he let go. The man went down as if clubbed, and another figure, this one heavier, crossed the bar of light, heading not for the street but the pile of lumber on the other side of the drive. This would be Ernie, and Chris shot again, and heard his buckshot slap into the stacked boards. He ran now for this stack of lumber, his gun under his arm, his good hand fumbling for fresh shells in his pocket.

He rounded the pile of lumber between it and the fence, and at the other end he saw the bright flame of a six-gun. Ducking back around the pile, he slipped two fresh loads in his gun, and now two more shots came. The top board of the pile boomed hollowly and slithered off the pile, crashing at his feet.

When the noise of it had died, he heard the pounding of running feet, and he knew Ernie was racing for the rear fence. Wheeling now, he ran down the center drive, passing the ghostly stacks of lumber looming above him. He had counted Ernie's shots, and, supposing Ernie had shot first, he had only one or, at best, two cartridges left. Ernie with his crippled hand would have the same trouble loading his gun as Chris did, and Chris was counting on that.

He came to the last stack of lumber, with the rear fence beyond, and he ran around its corner. There was no welcoming shot, and he hauled up, listening. He heard the faint grunt of a man and the scraping and slipping of boots on boards, and he guessed immediately that Ernie was trying to scale the fence.

Chris raised his gun and ran now toward the corner of the lot, peering through the rain into the darkness.

He saw a black bulk against the fence near to the corner, and he hauled up and called, "I've got a sight on your back, Ernie."

"I quit, damn you! I quit!" Ernie called in an angry, muffled voice. Chris heard him drop to the ground, and then he moved slowly forward.

Ernie stood motionless, his hands shoulder high, his bandage white in the darkness, as Chris approached him. Close now, Chris saw he was hatless, and his heavy breathing was the only sound in the slow rain.

Chris said then, for the second time that night, "You know where you're going. Go on."

The gate was open when they approached it, and a dozen men were clustered around the fallen man. From out of the gloom behind one of the stacks of lumber, O'Hea emerged, and wordlessly fell in beside Chris.

The crowd parted for the three of them, and Chris hauled up and looked down at the man lying on the ground. It was Bill Arnold. The shot had caught him fair in the back, in a spread of shot that a man's hand could cover, and he was dead.

Ernie had halted, too, and now he looked up at Chris and said thinly, "There's other people got shotguns here, too, Danning."

O'Hea led the way back to the jail. Chris cleared the corridor of a few curious stragglers, and Ernie stood defiantly impassive while O'Hea opened the cell door. Shallis watched from his cot.

Leach had come off his. Now, as the cell door swung open for Ernie, he snarled, "Keep that damn murderer away from me! I ain't a killer and I won't sleep with a pair of killers. I want a lawyer! I want Mrs. Harms!"

Chris saw Ernie's bleached eyes come alert, and he knew the damage was done. Leach had been warned, and he had not heeded it.

Chris went back into the corridor and persuaded the stragglers that the excitement was over, and then O'Hea came up behind him under the lamp. The old man said, "There's a cot I'll put just inside the door. You get some sleep, son."

Chris said, "Did you hear Leach?"

"I heard him," O'Hea said grimly. "That means he'll stay locked up till the trial, along with Ernie and Shallis."

They bid each other good night, and Chris, wet and tired, stepped out onto the boardwalk. Waycross' store across the street was lighted, which meant that Bill Arnold was being laid out in a back room alongside the man he had helped kill. The thought brought little comfort to Chris. He passed the lumberyard, and had mounted the first step of the outside stairs to his room above the barber shop when he halted.

There was something he had yet to do tonight, something he remembered only now. He went on upstreet now in the warm rain, which had soaked through his shirt. In anticipation of the inevitable mud, Hughie Melaven had had his swampers lay planks across the road at all four corners, and Chris stepped onto the plank that gave onto the boardwalk under the hotel veranda. There was a light in the hotel lobby, and he went in.

Fred Musgrove was standing in a corner of the lobby, talking to Kate as Chris stepped in. Fred ceased talking then, and touched his hat, and went out, passing Chris and bidding him good night. Chris noticed his shirt was wet, and surmised Fred had told Kate of tonight's happenings. He passed a pair of punchers waiting for the northbound stage who were snoring, hats over faces, on one of the big lounges, and went up to Kate.

"I wanted you to know I took your advice today," he said quietly. "I am O'Hea's deputy."

Kate smiled faintly. "I think that news has got around by now, Chris," she said gently, but there was pleasure reflected in her face. She said then, "Why did you take my advice?"

"I've been wondering that. Maybe because you were right about why I am here."

"You admit that?"

Chris only nodded, and Kate said, "I wish I had known you before this happened to you."

Chris frowned. "Why would you?"

"Because you're a kind man underneath. It shows through your selfishness once in a while."

Chris said, with a faint irony, "You seem to know a lot about me, Kate."

"Good men go wrong the same way," Kate said quietly. "I know all about you I need to know, except the beginning. I even know the end."

Chris looked at her a long moment. "And what is the end?"

"You'll kill him."

Chris said nothing, and Kate, watching him closely, said with a sudden intuitiveness, "It's beyond that that's troubling you, is it? I don't know that, Chris. You'll have to get it over with and see." She waited for him to speak, and when he did not, she said, "Good night," and left him.

He went on back downstreet and climbed the stairs to his bare room, which held only an iron bedstead, a washstand and a chair.

Stripping off his shirt, he changed to a fresh one, and then, sitting on the edge of his bed, he painstakingly rolled four cigarettes and put them on the chair which held the lamp by his bed; and all the time Kate's words were running through his mind, troubling him. How had she guessed he was wondering what lay beyond the death of Miles for him, when he had not known himself that he was wondering. Yet he had been. Suddenly the thought came to him, *Maybe I want to be free of this,* and the fact that he had even thought it shamed him.

He lighted his cigarette and lay back on the bed, and now, again, he turned his thoughts purposely to Bess. He found himself, without wanting to, comparing Bess with Kate. The two were alike in only a few things; not in looks, not in voice, not in figure. Bess was taller—or was she? He tried hard to remember, and could not, and a slow helpless bafflement came to him. How was it he could forget the thing he had sworn never to forget, even if he lived forever? And the thought came to him then, *Maybe you're beginning to want to forget them. They're part of a ghost, aren't they?*

He lay there, denying this to himself until he slept, the first cigarette cold in his fingers.

Chapter XVIII

The rain still held, slow and steady, when Mac crossed the bridge over the brawling Coroner into Rainbow around midday. The house, it seemed, was cold and deserted, and the cluster of hands in the bunkhouse doorway told MacElvey that Miles was not home yet from the tie camp. The leaderless crew greeted him as he dismounted, and one of them took his horse while the others questioned him. He told them of Bill Arnold's death, and of the arrest of Ernie and Shallis, and when he was finished they looked to him for leadership. He counseled them to wait for Miles.

A half hour later, with the crew milling and yarning behind him in the bunkhouse, Mac was standing in the doorway, listening idly to the Coroner. The runoff from the creeks had deepened its roar, and occasionally he could hear the rumble of the boulders rolling along the bottom. He was standing thus when he heard the sound of hoofbeats on the plank bridge and looked up to see Miles, riding his black, come off the bridge.

Mac stepped out into the mire of the lot and crossed it and was waiting under the tree by the picket fence as Younger, bulky in his slicker, rode up and dismounted. His square face was ruddy, his mustache wet, and now his expression was one of concern as he stepped out of the saddle. "Anything wrong, Mac?"

MacElvey told him of the death of Andy, the arrest of Shallis and of Danning's shooting of Arnold and capture of Ernie. As he talked, the crew began to drift across through the rain to them, but Younger paid them no attention. Mac was watching Miles' face as he told him of the conversation with Ernie this morning, in which Ernie said he was sure that Leach Conover had been a witness to the shooting of Andy West.

231

Younger was only smiling faintly, and his dark eyes held an angry amusement as Mac finished. "So O'Hea's got them in his jail, has he?" he observed mildly. He thought a moment, and then turned to a pair of the crew standing in the rain near by. "Arch, ride in and hitch up the big freight wagon. Three teams. Have it in the alley behind the store. . . . Saul, you go in with him. Cruise around town and find Danning and keep an eye on him. Take Ed with you, and send him back to me at the store when you locate him. The rest of you drift into town in pairs, so you'll be on hand. This time," he added grimly, "we get Danning."

A half hour later, with the three men preceding them, Mac and Younger left for town. Younger, strangely, was full of talk, none of it about Danning. Brush had started to move the road crew to Petrie this morning. Flanders had been sent on last night to Moorehouse to dispatch the telegrams. Things were rolling, Younger said. Danning, Mac thought, might have already been dead, for all the concern Younger showed.

As they passed the turnoff to Box H they saw a rider approaching. It was Della Harms, Younger said, and she dropped in a quarter mile behind them, taking the road to town.

The street was mired in mud as they reined up in front of the store in late afternoon, and it was still raining. Mac took the reins of Younger's horse and rode across the street and through the runway of the livery and turned the horses over to the hostler. When he turned to tramp back through the runway, he saw the slickered figure of Chris Danning, back to him, standing just inside the big doorway out of the rain. Danning was looking downstreet, and when he heard Mac he turned.

His gray eyes were cold and speculative, Mac saw, and Mac nodded and received a curt nod in return. As he passed him, Mac said in a low voice, not looking at him, "They're after you, friend. Watch yourself."

He kept on, crossing the deep mud to the store and went inside. Younger, a clerk said, was out on the loading platform in the rear. Mac stepped out the back door onto the sheltered loading platform. The big high-sided freight wagon, with its hitch of three teams, was pulled alongside the platform, and Younger was heaving a length of logging chain into the bed as Mac stepped out. Arch Morley, on the seat, was watching him with a puzzled expression. Ed Rossiter was looking on, too, and now Younger turned to him. "Go get horses for Ernie and Stew."

He saw Mac and grinned faintly, almost mischievously, and then said to Arch, "Pull around the block, Arch, and come in the alley behind the Masonic Hall."

Arch looked mystified, but he cursed the six wet horses into movement. Younger waited until he'd pulled past, then vaulted down into the mud and started up the alley, which made a right-angled turn at the juncture of Miles' store and Melaven's saloon. Passing the open gates of the lumber yard, he looked in, remembering Mac's account of the fight here last night. Beyond, there was a crate against the fence which partially blocked the alley, and he moved it against a shed opposite. Afterward, he waited in the rain for Arch, whistling thinly, his back against the jail wall.

Presently Arch turned into the alley and pulled up where Younger signaled him to stop. Younger got the chain from the wagon bed and looped one end of it around the wagon's heavy rear axle where it met the main brace. Now, with the hook end of the chain in hand, he climbed onto the tall rear wheel and then onto the high sideboard of the wagon, and Arch watched him. Still mystified. At this height Younger was level with the barred window. Playing out the chain until there was a foot of it extending from his hand, he slashed at the glass in the window, and it broke with a musical jingle.

Younger spoke into the jail, then. "Stand away, boys. You'll be out in a minute."

He looped the chain around the three bars and pulled the hook end back to him and hooked it in one of the links. Then he stepped down into the wagon bed, swung up beside Arch, and took the reins. Bracing his feet, he slashed savagely at the wheel horses and whistled shrilly.

The horses bolted, and Younger looked around just in time to see the chain rise out of the mud and tauten. There was a savage wrench and the back end of the wagon skidded around; then there was a splintering crash as the bars pulled out, taking six feet of the studding and siding of the building with them. The whole tangle of iron bars, window frame, two-by-four studding and shreds of the board siding landed in the alley with a crash and was dragged along by the chain.

Younger didn't even wait to fight the horses quiet. He flung the reins to Arch and vaulted to the alley, slipping and falling and quickly regained his feet.

Ernie Coombs was first out. He dropped the five feet to the alley, cradling his bandaged hand against his side, and ran toward Younger. Shallis followed him.

Ernie's bruised face was grinning, but there was something else there too. He halted by Younger and said, "Give me your gun, Younger."

"What for?"

"It ain't your neck," Ernie said sharply. "Give it to me."

Younger handed him his gun, and while he was doing it, he looked up to see Leach jump from the gaping hole to the alley, slip in the mud, regain his feet, and start to run in the opposite direction up the alley toward the Coroner.

Ernie palmed up the gun and took after him. He ran until he was almost even with Leach, then raised the gun and fired. Leach went flat on his face in the mud of the alley, and even at this distance Younger could hear the breath driven from him. Ernie stood over him a second, then tramped back. Younger noticed his pale hair was already beginning to mat with the slow rain, and when Ernie handed him the gun, Younger said,

"No witnesses this time, eh?"

"That's right," Ernie said quietly.

Shallis was looking at Leach, and he said nothing.

They unhooked the chain and climbed in the wagon and Arch drove down the alley, turned at the loading platform and pulled up.

Ed was waiting there with two saddled horses, and Mac, silent and watchful, stood just out of the rain. Younger vaulted out of the wagon and, handing six-guns to Ernie and Shallis, said to Mac, "Where is he?"

Ed said, "Saul says he's talkin' to Della Harms in the livery door."

"All right," Younger said grimly. "Ernie, you take Ed and circle around and come in past Melaven's. Stew, you take Saul and go down the alley and come in below him. I'll take him from the store side."

Ernie stepped into the saddle and then reined up his horse and said to all of them, "Wait a minute. He likes a shotgun so damn good." He looked at Mac. "Mac, get me a Greener and shells. Buckshot. Will you?"

Mac went back into the store and walked across it to the gun counter. Stooping, he reached below the counter and brought up a box of brass-cased shells, which he broke out. He laid two of them on the counter, took a knife from his pocket, and, in plain sight of a waiting customer, he dug out the wadding of the two shells and emptied the buckshot into his pocket. Afterward, he slipped the two shells into the gun, said to the customer, "Be with you in a minute," and went out the rear door with the gun.

He handed Ernie the gun, and Ernie said, "Where are the shells?"

"In there. I loaded it. Do you want more?"

Ernie clumsily half broke the gun with his left hand until he saw the rims of the two loads.

Younger said with a savage impatience, "Two's enough to kill him. You can't load it with that crippled hand anyway!"

Ernie snapped the breech shut, and shoved the shotgun in the saddle scabbard. "Ready," he said, and his horse was moving.

Chris watched MacElvey until he disappeared in the store, and then he thought, *He wrote the note*. Here, then, was Miles' traitor, and Chris knew the warning was real.

He looked downstreet then, his glance again on Della. From the hotel veranda, he had seen her on the edge of town, and remembering his errand, had come up to the livery.

She was wearing a man's oversize slicker, and when she dismounted just inside the door and said, "Hello, Chris," almost shyly, she seemed somehow appealing. The rain had brought a high color to her cheeks, and her broad-brimmed Stetson was dark with the rain. She smiled uncertainly at him, as if she were not quite sure of his friendship now, and said, "I hear you're O'Hea's new deputy." When he nodded, she said soberly, "Then it was you Leach saw? I sent him in last night, and he isn't home yet."

237

"Leach," Chris said quietly, "is in jail."

Della looked searchingly at him, and he regarded her levelly. "Why?" Della asked. "He didn't kill Andy."

"Not in the way you mean. He killed him by talking your mother into jumping Tip Henry's homestead." He paused. "I've put him away until I could talk to you."

Della said quietly, "Why don't you blame me for sending Andy up there? I made him go."

"Leach started it, and he's to blame," Chris said grimly. "Get rid of him, Della."

Della unaccountably turned her back to him and put her hand to her eyes. It took Chris a moment to realize she was crying, and he stood there baffled, sorry for her, knowing there was nothing he could do to help her. She was a girl without iron, without stability, impetuous one moment, sorry for what her impetuosity had cost in the next. There was no comfort he could give her, and he said nothing. Suddenly, above the muffled sound of her sobbing, he heard a shot from a six-gun. It came from somewhere behind the buildings in the opposite block, and he supposed some puncher, full of whisky and the boredom of the long rain, was easing his feelings.

And Della cried, softly, heartbrokenly, still holding the reins of her wet chestnut. It was minutes before Chris, taciturnly regarding the street, heard her say, "Chris, will you come back?"

He turned and looked at her, surprising a look of

naked longing in her eyes that shocked him. He moved his head once in negation. "I can't, Della."

"Is it because of what I said?" Della asked swiftly. "I was wrong, Chris. I've been judging you as if you were the man I talked to the first day. You aren't. Won't you come back?"

Chris looked levelly at her. "It wouldn't work, Della."

She nodded and silently stroked the nose of her horse. Presently, she said in a musing voice, "I'm growing up I guess. Nothing will be the same again. I used to love Leach. Yordy was funny, and a grand and dashing gent. And I used to tease Andy to make him blush. I was mean to him, like kids can be mean to a dog they know won't bite them."

Chris wasn't listening now; he had seen Younger Miles come out of the store and look upstreet, then downstreet. Something in his manner made Chris look downstreet too. He saw Stew Shallis and another rider coming down the street, watching the livery. Looking upstreet he saw Ernie Coombs and a strange rider at the intersection, and he knew that Miles had got them out of jail, and that this was it. Even as his glance shuttled back to the store, he saw Miles vaulting down the steps, clawing at the gun in his belt.

Chris moved, then. He shoved Della roughly out of the way behind the big sliding door, and grabbed the reins of her horse and vaulted into the saddle. Miles shot first, and Chris heard his shot hit the planks and ricochet in a singing whine out the rear door. He pulled Della's chestnut around and, leaning over its neck, he roweled him down the livery runway toward the rear door, and heard Miles' voice, wild with wrath, yelling, "Cut him off! Cut him off!"

Chris passed the corral in back, hearing a horse thundering into the entrance of the livery, and he pulled his gun and swerved left into the alley, heading instinctively in the direction of the Blackbows.

He had gone only a few yards down the alley when Shallis cut into the alley dead ahead of him. He saw Chris and tried to pull up his horse, and raised his gun. Chris shot twice, and saw the horse, already in a rear, take the hit and go over backwards, and then he swerved right between two sheds, just as the rider behind him opened up. He was in the back yard of a mean little shack, and he cut angling across its greasy, rain-pooled mud. The chestnut stumbled on the slippery boardwalk bisecting the yard and recovered, and then Chris saw the clothesline ahead of him. He ducked flat on the back of his horse and the line raked his back, and then he put his horse in between two houses just as a second shot slammed into the wall of the far house. Swerving the chestnut to keep from running into a child's wagon, he cut across the front yard and was in the street, which petered out onto the flats ahead.

He looked behind him now, and saw it was Ernie Coombs, still bareheaded, who was behind him, close, and he turned and raised his gun and shot. With his left hand and on horseback, his shooting was wild, and he missed, and he could almost see the expression of cold ferocity on Ernie's face as his horse hit the street now and took after him.

His chestnut was in a dead gallop, and when they had left the edge of town and were on the muddy flats, Chris knew the chestnut couldn't take it. Looking back, he saw three riders strung out far behind Ernie who was gaining on him. The chestnut, Chris knew, had been ridden from Box H today, and would play out soon.

As if to punctuate his thought, he heard Ernie shoot. Chris turned in the saddle, and tried again, and again his shooting was bad; and only after that did he realize that his gun was empty.

He tried, fumbling, to reload, reins over his injured hand, body bent low in the saddle. But he could not fumble the shells from his shell belt, and when he did finally, he could not with one hand force them in the loading gate.

He looked back now and saw that Ernie had pulled a shotgun or rifle from the saddle scabbard, and Chris knew with a gray and hateful certainty that he was cornered unless he could load his gun.

Looking ahead in the fading light of dusk, he made out the distant bulk of Briggs' place. If he could make that, and contrive to dodge in the tangle of those corrals for the few precious moments it would take to load his gun, he might make it.

Chapter XIX

Younger's black, which he hauled from the livery corral and mounted bareback in his haste to take part in the chase, quit on him a mile out on the flats. He simply slacked into a walk and then stopped, and only quivered when Younger raked him with his spurs in a fury of impatience. The horse had carried him from the tie camp to Triumph today, and he could not work more. It took Younger only a moment to acknowledge this, and he let the black blow a few moments, and then turned back to town, his temper ugly and wild. As he came up to the livery stable and dismounted he saw a knot of onlookers gathered at the big livery door, and O'Hea was among them. They were standing just out of the rain.

Younger swung down and flipped his reins to the hostler and O'Hea said quietly, "Come along, Younger. You're under arrest."

Younger stood motionless in the rain, looking over the small crowd. He counted eight Rainbow hands among them, and then he looked at O'Hea.

"What did I do now?"

"Broke Ernie and Shallis out of jail."

"So where do you put me until you get it fixed?" Younger asked mockingly. He looked the crowd over now, his eyes bold and unafraid, and then he glanced at O'Hea. "Any offense is bailable, short of murder, according to your sheriff's book, isn't it?"

O'Hea nodded.

"Then figure out what you want from me and get the bail from Truscott," Younger said bluntly. "I'm busy and you always know where to find me."

He turned his back to O'Hea and, with a magnificent disdain, started across the muddy road. A half dozen Rainbow hands broke from the crowd and followed him, and O'Hea, helpless, watched him go.

On the steps of the store Younger paused and turned to his men. "Arch, you hang around the livery. Maybe Ernie and the boys will miss Danning and he'll come back."

He went on in the store now, his slicker dripping a thin line of water down the aisle. The lamps were already lighted against the gloom of early evening, and Younger went on back to the office.

Mac was engaged in conversation with a small scholarly-looking man of middle age whom Younger recognized as Travis, the surveyor he had hired.

They stopped talking at Younger's entrance, and rose, and Younger, halting, said in a puzzled voice to Travis, "I thought Mac sent you to Petrie."

"I just rode in from Petrie, Mr. Miles," Travis said coldly. "There's been a mistake made somewhere along the line. Mr. MacElvey gave me to understand that you people were low bidders on that freight contract, and that I was to start the road survey immediately."

"That's right," Younger said. He was shucking out of his slicker.

"Then you'd better see Mr. Coe at Petrie. He's under the impression Farnum Brothers were low bidders. So are they. Their road crew is there, and the surveyors are already at work."

"Farnum Brothers?" Younger echoed blankly. "You say you saw Coe?" He let his slicker fall to the floor.

"I did."

"What did Coe say?" Younger demanded slowly.

"I told you. Farnum Brothers were low bidders. The contract was signed yesterday by Mr. Hardy, Sulinam's treasurer. I saw a copy of the contract."

Younger stared blankly at MacElvey, who shrugged. Younger strode over to the safe, pulled open the door and squatted long enough to unlock a drawer and pull out a letter. He came back, handed it to Travis, saying, "What does that read like to you?"

Travis read the letter. "A forgery," he said simply. "Hardy isn't east. He's in Coe's office probably at this very moment. That's not Coe's signature. Do you know it?"

"His signature? No," Miles said. "Do you, Mac?"

"No."

Travis put the letter on the desk, saying, "Farnum Brothers bid was some thirteen cents a ton less than your figure. I saw that, too."

Miles only stared at him with complete bafflement. He started to say something and did not, and he licked the corners of his lips slowly, looking at Travis.

"Somebody," Travis observed, "has played a very unfortunate trick on you, Mr. Miles. I can imagine your feelings. Nevertheless, I was somewhat inconvenienced myself. I—"

"Pay him," Younger said softly to Mac.

Mac asked the figure and Travis mentioned it, and Mac wrote out the check. Travis put out his hand to Miles, who was staring out the window, and Miles roused himself with an effort and shook hands. Then he stared again at the window as Travis went out.

A clerk came in and said, "I'll go to supper now, Mr. MacElvey," and Mac nodded and the clerk went out, closing the door behind him.

Mac went over to the letter and picked it up, and then he said quietly, "You better get a man over to Moorehouse with telegrams of cancellation, Younger. Save what you can."

"Who did it, Mac?" Younger asked quietly.

"I don't know. There's time to worry about that when you've saved what you can."

Miles grunted, looking at him. "You suppose Dan hasn't paid for the horses? You suppose our deposit on the wagons hasn't been paid by Sholtz, and the contract signed? You suppose that feed isn't bought and the first of it on its way? The harness bought? The crews signed up by Brush, the lumber bought, the deal closed on the blacksmith shop? The— Oh hell!"

Mac put down the letter and looked at Younger.

"Who did it, Mac?"

MacElvey shook his head. "The Sulinam letterhead is right. I've seen that. The names are right. The talk is right. The—"

"I've lost a fortune," Younger interrupted quietly. "You know that, Mac? I paid cash for everything, to stretch my money. I mortgaged Rainbow."

Mac nodded, and he and Younger stared at each other, and again Younger said, "Who did it?"

Mac shrugged, came up to him and said quietly, "Get a grip on yourself, Younger. Every minute we lose before we get telegrams off to Dan and Sholtz and the wagon outfit might be costing us money. Is everybody chasing Danning?"

Younger said absently, "Arch is at the livery."

"I'm going to send him over to Moorehouse, then. Is that all right?"

Again Younger nodded absently, and Mac left the office. The store was almost empty, for the supper hour was here, and only two clerks remained. Mac went down the steps and ducked under the hitch post and crossed the street to the livery in the rain. Just inside the door, Arch was sitting on a feed bin, talking with the hostler beside him.

Mac went up and said to him, "Got a gun with you, Arch?"

Arch nodded, and Mac put out his hand. "Younger wants it."

"What's the matter with his?" Arch asked, reaching for the six-gun holstered at his hip.

"Something happened to the hammer," Mac said quietly. "I don't know anything about guns."

Arch handed him his six-gun, which Mac took awkwardly by the barrel and started back across the street with it. His attention was attracted by someone standing by the outside door of the livery office in the rain, and when he glanced over, he saw it was Kate Hardison, and he halted.

"Have they got him, Mac?" Kate asked slowly.

"No," Mac said, and then he added in a kindly voice, "Get out of the rain, Kate."

She turned wordlessly and went back in the direction of the hotel. Mac, out of sight of Arch now, opened his vest and rammed the gun in his belt and buttoned his vest again. By that time he was inside the store; he shook the rain from his coat and went on through to the office.

The closest building to Chris on Briggs' place as he came on it now was a high corral and he dismissed this instantly. It would have to be the shack, some solid thing that would give him protection in the lowering dusk while he took the precious time to reload.

Looking over his shoulder, he saw that Ernie had gained only a slight distance. It was too far for effective use of his shotgun, and Ernie, Chris knew, was risking everything on that. Ernie understood and knew, too, the stakes of the race, and he was riding low, urging the last burst of speed from his horse.

Chris already had the shells from his belt in his hand, and now as he rounded the tangle of corrals and headed for the house, he put them in his mouth. Della's chestnut tripped and stumbled, almost foundered and recovered just past the door of Briggs' sagging shack. Chris swung a leg over the saddle and, as he reached the far corner of the shack, he leaped clear. He slipped and fell in the mud and came to his knees, and ran for the corner of the shack. He held the six-gun, loading gate open, wedged in the hollow of his right arm, and patiently, slowly, tried to fumble in a cartridge, and then he heard Ernie's horse at a run. Chris' tracks in the mud were eloquent; Ernie would know where to look for him, and he was on him even now. A dismal gray taste of death was in Chris now. He rose and ran for the back of the shack, at last slipping in the single cartridge.

He heard Ernie's horse pound past the corner of the shack, and he saw Ernie leap from the saddle, gun in hand, just as he put the corner between them. Chris stopped then. He had the single load in. Awkwardly, desperately, he tried with his left hand to spin the cylinder, so that the cartridge would be under the hammer, and then he heard Ernie's pounding step and looked up.

Ernie rounded the corner at a run and hauled up, not eight feet away. He shot once from the hip, even before he halted, and Chris cringed away, waiting for the shot to take him. Nothing happened, except the sting of powder on his cheek. And now the cartridge was in place, and Chris cocked the gun and looked up as Ernie, his face savage and baleful, shot again.

And again came the powder sting and nothing more, and Chris, realizing he was unhit, took two solid steps toward Ernie and lifted his gun. Some wild instinct of survival moved Ernie to raise his gun as a club, and then Chris shot. The slug caught Ernie in the chest and he sat down abruptly and went flat on his back. He raised one knee and sighed, and his leg straightened out in the mud.

Chris stood there a still moment, shaking, humble with fear, before the slow realization came that the others, whom Ernie had widely outdistanced, were after him too. He stood in his tracks in the rain and loaded his gun, and then ran for Ernie's horse, which had stopped as soon as Ernie had left the saddle.

He mounted and put the horse at a reluctant trot past the shed, and was again out on the flats. Through the lowering dusk he saw the first of the riders a quarter mile on the other side of Briggs' dark shack. He rode steadily for a while, and when it was too dark to see any distance, he swung in a wide half circle toward the west. The others had lost him, or had been sobered by the finding of Ernie. Presently he made the full circle, and headed back toward Triumph, knowing that at last it was here. And oddly now, he thought of what lay beyond, and what Kate said to him last night: "You'll have to get it over with and see, Chris." He knew now that he wanted to live beyond what would happen next; he wanted to come out of it alive, and a year ago he hadn't cared.

He came into Triumph from the west, and turned in the alley alongside the hotel and dismounted in the rear of the livery. It was dark in the runway, and, framed against the lights from Miles' store across the street, Chris saw the hostler talking with another man. He was almost up to them when they heard him and turned. The tall man came off the grain chest, making a gesture for his gun, and then his hand ceased moving as Chris lifted his gun.

"You Rainbow?" Chris asked.

"Yes," Arch muttered.

Chris came up to him and saw that his holster was empty, and he said, "He in the store?"

Arch nodded, and Chris waved him toward the street with his gun.

The sound of a horse being ridden hard down the street came to them then, and Chris put an arm out and halted Arch. They watched a rider, coming from the direction of the flats, pull up in front of Miles' store, dismount hurriedly, and go inside.

He's bringing the news of Ernie, Chris thought.

The sound of someone upstreet running on the boardwalk came to him. And then he saw the figure cutting across the muddy street from the hotel in the direction of Miles' store. In that dim light, he made out Kate Hardison, small in a bulky slicker; and as she ran up the stairs and entered the store, his gray spirit lifted. *She cares enough to wonder what news he brought. She was watching,* he thought; and still he waited.

In a moment the rider came out of the store, hurried down the steps and turned in the direction of Melaven's saloon, and Chris supposed he was after help. Rainbow, most likely, would have their horses stalled out of the rain here at the livery. It was time to move.

"Go in the store," he said to Arch and the hostler, and together they walked across the street, mounted the steps and entered the store. It was deserted, save for a woman customer at the rear. The office door was closed, and Chris halted Arch and the hostler midway down the aisle and turned and listened. He picked up the sound of men running for the livery, and a minute later the first horse hit the planks of the runway at a run. In seconds the sound of the riders in the muddy street had died, and now Chris motioned Arch ahead and sent the hostler out.

As they approached the office door, Chris heard the voice of Miles from behind the partition, and it was cold with wrath.

"I'll hunt him down if it takes my crew a year. I'll hire another crew to hunt him down after that. Meddle somewhere else! Get out!"

Kate's voice was barely audible. "He's worth a hundred of that trash you've got hunting him."

"Get out, Kate."

"I make you a promise, Younger," Kate said. "If they get him, I'll kill you."

Younger laughed, and now Chris looked at Arch and motioned with his head toward the front door. Meekly, Arch turned and tramped out, and Chris watched him until he was out.

He heard Younger say now, "You like that drifter, don't you, Kate?" but the time was here for him. He tucked his gun under his right arm, softly turned the doorknob with his left, and when the door was ajar, he took his gun and gently shoved the door open with his foot and stepped in.

Kate and MacElvey were standing, their backs to him, and Younger was facing him. Younger was talking, his tone jeering, and now his voice trailed off and he closed his mouth. His face smoothed slowly, became slowly blank. Kate, seeing it, whirled, and Chris said gently, "Go out, Kate."

She fled past him, and he did not even look at Mac, only said, watching Miles, "Mac, I'm going to kill him. I don't think you'll stop me."

"Wait," Mac said.

"No," Chris said, still looking at Miles. "Before I kill you, Miles, I'm going to tell you why." He paused, isolating this. "There was a girl on that stage that Tana trapped in Karnes Canyon along with Captain Jordan's pay chest. They killed her. She was on her way to me, because we were going to be married."

Miles' face showed he was not even going to protest his innocence.

And then Mac's voice cut in, "Her name was Bess Thornley, Miles, and she was my sister."

Chris didn't take his glance from Miles as he heard this. He saw the fleeting amazement and terror come into Miles' face now, and he glanced swiftly at Mac and saw the gun in his hand, held down at his side.

Mac said, "I faked that letter from Coe, Miles. I'd worked a year to break you, and I did. I want you to know you're broke before you die."

He raised his gun slowly, and Younger backed into the safe. Then he wheeled and vaulted for the window. Mac shot then. Younger had one leg on the window sill, and the force of Mac's first shot drove him into the window, and it broke. Then he sagged to his knees, both hands clutching the window sill, and Mac shot him four times in the back, coldly and carefully.

Chris watched Miles fall to the floor between the desk and the safe, and wedge there grotesquely, knees to chin. Chris discovered his gun was still leveled, and he let it fall to his side, and when Mac, his face fiercely exultant, turned to him, Chris said, "You're Perry, then, and you have known who I was."

"Yes. Since I heard your name. I wanted to hurt him all I could before you killed him."

They both looked at Miles then, and Chris walked over to Mac's chair and sat down wearily. He leaned his elbows on his knees and rubbed his closed eyes with the rough palm of his hand; he was thinking, *I'm rid of you now, Bess. At last I'm rid of you.*

Mac said to him now, "So you got to Tana, too?"

"No. He was dead. I talked to one of the others." He looked briefly at Miles again, and said, "How did you find him?"

"He had to do something with his money," Mac said. "I tried a lot of things until I thought of the stockmen's journals. I went to the back issues and found mention of the sale of the Finch holdings to him. I changed my name, in case he ever discovered Bess had a brother."

Chris nodded and rose wearily. This was ended, and he knew suddenly the question neither he nor Kate could answer yesterday was ready to be answered now. He smiled slowly and put his hand on Mac's arm and pressed it, and went out into the store. A group of customers and clerks just outside the door parted for him, and he was shouldering through them when Mac called, "Chris." Chris stopped, and Mac said, "I want to be tried for this, but I'd like your permission to see Mrs. Miles before you take me to O'Hea."

"All right," Chris said. He went out and stepped down into the rain and cut straight across the deep mud toward the hotel. And then he saw the figure at the corner of the hotel, standing in the slow rain, watching him. It was Kate.

He came up to her then, and she said quietly, "He's dead, Chris?"

Chris nodded his head in slow affirmation. "He's dead, and I didn't kill him, Kate, and it's over. She's gone, she's buried, and I'm done with it. I'm—" He paused, realizing she did not know what he was talking about.

"You don't have to tell me, Chris."

"I want to," Chris said. "I want to tell you more, Kate. I want to—" Again he stopped, reaching for the words, and she looked up at him, her face grave and waiting.

He touched her face gently with his hand and said, "Blessed Kate," knowing that she could wait for the other words.

Center Point Publishing
600 Brooks Road ● PO Box 1
Thorndike ME 04986-0001 USA

(207) 568-3717

US & Canada:
1 800 929-9108

CARVG 04/10

LGH	*May 07,* Sept 07
SIL	
H	
KCC	*Apr 07*
W	
CED	*Sep 07*

CED	
KCC	
LB	
LGH	*may 11*
SUN	
W	
Z	